Crimson Twilight

A Krewe of Hunters Novella

By Heather Graham

1001 Dark Nights

EVIL EYE
CONCEPTS

Crimson Twilight
A Krewe of Hunters Novella
1001 Dark Nights
By Heather Graham

On the Krewe of Hunters
By Heather Graham

I've always been fascinated by both history and stories that had elements that were eerie and made us wonder what truly goes on, what is the human soul—and is there life after death? When I was young, I devoured gothic novels and became a fan of Washington Irving, Edgar Allan Poe, Bram Stoker's *Dracula* and Mary Shelley's *Frankenstein*.

And with years passing—for some of us earlier in life and others later—we lose people. When we lose people, we have to believe that we'll see them again, that there is a Heaven or an afterlife. Sometimes, it's the only true comfort we have. I think it's a beautiful part of us—the love we can have for others. But it also allows for pain so deep it can't be endured unless we have that belief that we can and will meet again.

Having grown up with a Scottish father and an Irish mother, I naturally spent some time in church learning the Nicene Creed—in which we vow that we believe in the Holy Ghost.

I suppose people with very mathematical and scientific minds can easily explain away such things as "death" experiences shared by many who technically died on operating tables before being brought back. "Neurons snapping in the brain," is one explanation I've heard.

But I sadly lack a scientific brain and my math is pathetic, so I choose to believe that all things may be possible.

Have I ever sat down with a ghost myself? No.

But I have been many places where it's easy to imagine that the dead might linger. I've heard of many strange tales. And I love the chance that when a loved one needs to be soothed, when a right must be avenged, a ghost—or perhaps the strength and energy of the human soul—might remain.

Thus the Krewe.

Who better than an offshoot of a crime-fighting agency to help these wronged individuals—far too, well, *dead*, themselves—who wish to set the record straight?

I've had incredible chances myself to do wonderful things and while I haven't met a ghost, I have certainly been places where the very air around you feels different. Walking through the Tower of London, stepping into Westminster Cathedral—or standing at dusk on one of the hallowed fields of Gettysburg, you can easily feel seeped with history and the lives that went before us.

I've enjoyed working on the Krewe novels, setting them various places I've loved myself. Each year, a group of writers takes the Lizzie Borden house for a night. For promo, I've done a documented séance at the House of the Seven Gables. I've been on expeditions with ghost "hunters" on the Queen Mary, the Spanish Military Hospital, the Myrtles Plantation, and many more wonderful locations where history, time, and place took their toll on men and women.

Wonderfully fun things happen. The incredible owner of the Lizzie Borden Bed and Breakfast and Museum, has restored the house to as close to the way it looked the fateful day that Lizzie herself either did—or didn't—take an ax (or hatchet!) and give her mother forty whacks. (It was really somewhere between 18 and 20, but that doesn't work well in a rhyme!) One year, the Biography Channel was filming there and my newly graduated Cal-Arts actress daughter, Chynna Skye, played Lizzie Borden for the Biography Channel—and hacked me to pieces as Abby Borden. (What a charming mother/daughter shot, right?) I've stayed at the 17hundred90 Inn in Savannah in the room from which their resident ghost, Anne, pitched to her death. The management there has a wonderful sense of humor—they have a mannequin of Anne in one of the windows, waving to those on the tours that go by. We also happened to follow a then young recording and television star's stay in the room. She left the inn a letter, telling them that Anne had been in her luggage, messing up all her packing. Having spent time with ghost trackers who did seek the logical explanation first, all I could think was, "But did you look for the note from the TSA?"

A favorite occasion was at the Spanish Military Hospital in St. Augustine where, watching the cameras set up by my friends, the Peace River Ghost Trackers, I was certain I saw a ghost. But good ghost trackers are out to find the solid solution to a "haunting" first—it was pointed out to me that I was seeing Scott's shadow as he moved across the room.

While Adam Harrison first makes his appearance in *Haunted*, the Krewe of Hunters series actually begins with *Phantom Evil*, taking place in one of my favorite cities in the world, New Orleans, Louisiana. I have put on a writers' conference there every year since the awful summer of storms and flooding decimated the city. There are few places in the world with an aura of "faded elegance," of the past being an integral part of the present. There are tales of courage there, of tragedy, and of adventure. The cemeteries stir the imaginations of the most solid thinkers. There are many ghosts with the right to be truly furious at their earthly fates—not to mention some of the most delicious food in the world!

Jane Everett and Sloan Trent first meet during a wicked season of murder at an old theater in Arizona reminiscent of the Bird Cage. The Wild, Wild, West certainly had its share of violence and intrigue as well. Cultures came together and clashed, miners sought treasure, and the ever-present human panorama of life went on—including love gone wrong, hatred, jealousy, and greed.

And where ghosts might well linger. If they exist, of course.

For this story—while thankfully, nothing went wrong and it was an incredibly beautiful day!—I have chosen a castle in New England and the seed of its imagining came from a real wedding—my son's.

Yes, in America, we have castles. That's because we've had men who lived with massive fortunes and could indulge their whims and have them brought over—brick by brick or stone by stone—from a European country. And there's just something about a castle...

So many things can go wrong at a wedding. What with dresses, a wedding party, nervous brides, nervous grooms, bad caterers, and so on.

But what could be worse than the minister—dead on the morning of the nuptials?

Dedication

For Franci Naulin and D.J. Davant

Yevgeniya Yeretskaya and Derek Pozzessere

and

Alicia Ibarra and Robert Rosello

And to all kinds of different, beautiful—wonderful weddings!

One Thousand and One Dark Nights

Once upon a time, in the future…

*I was a student fascinated with stories and learning.
I studied philosophy, poetry, history, the occult, and
the art and science of love and magic. I had a vast
library at my father's home and collected thousands
of volumes of fantastic tales.*

*I learned all about ancient races and bygone
times. About myths and legends and dreams of all
people through the millennium. And the more I read
the stronger my imagination grew until I discovered
that I was able to travel into the stories... to actually
become part of them.*

*I wish I could say that I listened to my teacher
and respected my gift, as I ought to have. If I had, I
would not be telling you this tale now.
But I was foolhardy and confused, showing off
with bravery.*

*One afternoon, curious about the myth of the
Arabian Nights, I traveled back to ancient Persia to
see for myself if it was true that every day Shahryar
(Persian: شهریار, "king") married a new virgin, and then
sent yesterday's wife to be beheaded. It was written
and I had read, that by the time he met Scheherazade,*

the vizier's daughter, he'd killed one thousand women.

Something went wrong with my efforts. I arrived in the midst of the story and somehow exchanged places with Scheherazade — a phenomena that had never occurred before and that still to this day, I cannot explain.

Now I am trapped in that ancient past. I have taken on Scheherazade's life and the only way I can protect myself and stay alive is to do what she did to protect herself and stay alive.

Every night the King calls for me and listens as I spin tales. And when the evening ends and dawn breaks, I stop at a point that leaves him breathless and yearning for more. And so the King spares my life for one more day, so that he might hear the rest of my dark tale.

As soon as I finish a story... I begin a new one... like the one that you, dear reader, have before you now.

Chapter One

"I say we fool around again," Sloan Trent said.

Jane Everett smiled.

They'd spent the night before fooling around—even though it had been their wedding eve— so she assumed they'd fool around again a great deal tonight.

Which was nothing new for them.

They'd finally made it out of the shower and into clothing and were ready to head downstairs. But Sloan was still in an amorous mood. He drew her to him, kissed her neck just below her ear, and whispered, "There's so much time in life that we can't fool around... so you have to fool around when the fooling around is good, right?" He had that way of whispering against her ear. His breath was hot and moist and somehow had a way of creating little fires that trickled down into her sex, generating an instant burst of desire.

"We've just showered," she reminded him.

"Showers can be fun, too."

"We're supposed to be meeting up with Kelsey and Logan and seeing a bit of the castle before we get ready for the ceremony."

"You never know. Maybe Logan and Kelsey are fooling around and showering, too?"

He pressed his lips to her throat and her collarbone, drawing her closer, making the spoon of their bodies into something erotic.

She wasn't sure what would have happened if it hadn't been for the scream.

More a shriek!

Long, loud, piercing, horrible.

They broke apart, both of them making mad leaps for the Glock firearms they were never without, racing out of their room to the upper landing of the castle's staircase. Of all the things Jane hadn't expected as her wedding approached, it was for the minister to be found dead—neck broken, eyes-wide-open—at the first floor landing of Castle Cadawil. Logan Raintree and Kelsey O'Brien, their co-workers and witnesses for the wedding, rushed up close behind them.

They all paused, assessing the situation, then raced down.

Reverend Marty MacDonald lay on his back, head twisted at that angle which clearly defined death, his legs still on the steps, arms extended as if he'd tried to fly. Sloan looked at her, shaking his head sadly. She felt as if all the air had been sucked from her lungs. Her blood began to run cold. Her first thought was for Marty MacDonald. She didn't know him that well. She'd met and hired him here, on the New England coast, just a month ago when she'd first seen the castle. She and Sloan had been talking about what to do and how and when to marry, and it had suddenly seemed right.

But now. The poor man!

Her next thought was—

Oh, God! What did this say for their lives together? What kind of an omen—

"Tripped?" Logan Raintree suggested, studying the dead man and the stairs.

Logan was the leader of the Texas Krewe of Hunters—the mini-division within their special unit of the FBI. Many of their fellow agents liked to attach the word "special" with a mocking innuendo, but for the most part the Bureau looked upon them with a fair amount of respect. They were known for coming up with results. Jane had known Logan a long time. They were both Texans and had worked with Texas law enforcement before they'd joined on with the Krewe.

Kelsey had come into it as a U.S. Marshal. She'd been working in Key West, her home stomping grounds, until she'd been called to Texas on a serial murder case. She and Logan had been a twosome ever since. One weekend they'd slipped away and quietly married. They told no one and it had become a pool in the home office, had they or hadn't they? If so, when?

Sloan had profited $120 with his guess. Sloan wasn't a Texan, though he, too, had worked there. Jane had met Sloan in Arizona during the curious case of the deaths at the Gilded Lily. He'd been acting-sheriff there at the time. Six-foot-four, broad-shouldered, wearing a badge and a Stetson, he'd been pretty appealing. That case put some distance and resentment between them, until solving it drew them together in a way that would never end.

"Tripped?" Logan said again, and she caught the question in his voice.

Logan and Sloan, and all of the members of the Krewe, worked well together. Logan and Sloan both had Native American mixes in their backgrounds, which brought a sense and respect for all beliefs and all possibilities.

Jane loved that about both men.

Of course, she loved Kelsey, too. She'd known Kelsey her whole life. Having grown up in the Florida Keys, Kelsey also had a keen interest in everyone and everything. She was bright, blonde, and beautiful, ready to tackle anything.

"So it appears," Kelsey murmured.

"Did you see anyone?" Sloan asked the maid, whose horrified scream had alerted them all.

The maid shook her head.

"I'm trying to picture," Sloan said, "how he tripped and

ended up here, as he is."

"He had to have come down from far up," Kelsey noted.

Sloan rose and started up the winding stone stairway. "He'd have had to have tripped at the top of the stairs, rolled, and actually tumbled down to this position."

"Anyone can trip," Kelsey said, laying a hand on Jane's arm. "I'm so sorry."

Jane closed her eyes for a minute. She wanted to believe it. Tripped. A sad accident. Marty MacDonald had been a loner, a bachelor without any exes to mourn him and no children or grandchildren to miss their dad or grandpa. But did that mitigate a human life?

The housekeeper who'd screamed was still standing, staring down at the corpse through glazed eyes, her mouth locked into a circle of horror.

Jane felt frozen herself.

They were used to finding the dead. That was their job. Called in when unexplained deaths and circumstances came about. But this was her minister—the man who was to have married her and Sloan. She didn't move. The others still seemed to have their wits about them. She heard Sloan dialing 911 and speaking in low, even tones to the dispatch officer. Soon, there would be sirens. A medical examiner would arrive. The police would question them all. Naturally, it looked like an accidental death. But Jane always doubted accidental death.

But that was in her nature.

Would the police doubt so, too?

She felt a sense of hysteria rising inside her. She could wind up in an interrogation room on the other side of the table. *Did you do this? I think I know what happened,"* a hard-boiled detective right out of some dime novel would demand. He'd be wearing a Dick Tracey hat and trench coat. *"What was it? You were afraid of commitment. Afraid of marriage. You don't really love that poor bastard, Sloan, do you? You didn't think you'd get away with killing the rugged cowboy type of man he is. Tall, strong, always impossibly right. So you killed the minister. Pushed a poor innocent man of God right down the stairs!"*

Whoa.

Double whoa.

She didn't feel that way. She'd never felt for anyone like she did for Sloan. She was in love with his mind, his smile, his voice. The way he was with her, and the way he was with the world. They shared that weirdness of their special ability to speak with the dead. They also shared a need to use their gift in the best way. She definitely loved him physically. He was rugged and weathered, a cowboy, tall and broad-shouldered, everything a Texas girl might have dreamed about. He had dark hair, light eyes, sun-bronzed features, and a smile that could change the world.

Except that he wasn't smiling now.

"You just now found him?" Sloan asked the maid.

The woman didn't respond.

"Ms. Martin," Sloan pressed.

Jane had noticed the maid's nametag too, identifying her as Phoebe Martin. At last, the woman blinked, focused, and turned to Sloan, nodding sadly, like a child admitting an obvious but unhappy fact.

"Is anyone else here?" Sloan asked her. "I mean, besides you, me, Logan, Kelsey, and Jane?" He pointed around to all of them, using their first names. That was a way to make her feel comfortable, as if she were one with them. In situations like this, people spoke way more easily to authorities when they felt as if they were conversing with friends.

The maid, an attractive young blonde woman of about twenty-seven or so, shook her head. "Right here, no. I didn't see anybody. I was coming from the kitchen and saw him lying here. But, yes, yes, of course, others are around. They're always around. The castle is never left empty. The caretaker, Mr.

Green, is somewhere about."

"Anyone else?" Jane prodded gently.

Ms. Martin nodded solemnly. "Mrs. Avery is in her office along with Scully Adair, her assistant. And the chef came in about an hour or so ago. So did two of the cooks. Lila and Sonia are here. They're with housekeeping."

Jane knew that Mrs. Denise Avery managed the castle. She'd dealt with the woman to rent the rooms they'd taken for the weekend, including the chapel and ballroom. The castle was actually owned by a descendant of Emil Roth, the eccentric millionaire who, in the late 1850s, had the building disassembled in Wales and brought to the coastline of New England. The owner, another Emil Roth, had been born with more money than he'd been able to waste. The Roth family had made their fortune in steel, then banking. The current Roth was gone, Jane had been told, to Africa on a big game photography hunt. Mrs. Avery was a distant relative herself. And while the current Emil Roth spent money, Mrs. Avery tried to make it.

"Miss Martin, perhaps you could gather them all here, in the foyer," Sloan suggested.

"Gather them," she repeated.

"Yes, please, would you?" Jane prodded.

"The police and the coroner will arrive any minute and everyone should be here when they do," Sloan said.

Phoebe Martin looked at them at last. "Police?"

"A man is dead," he said. "Yes, the police."

"But… he… fell," she said.

"Possibly," Logan said.

"Probably," Jane said firmly.

Phoebe's eyes widened still further. "Pushed!"

"No. All we know is that he's dead," Jane said. "The local police need to come and the death investigated. The medical examiner or the coroner must come, too."

"Pushed!" Phoebe said again.

"There is that possibility," Kelsey said. She glanced at Jane and grimaced sorrowfully. "But, he probably just fell. No one was there, right? We were all in our rooms, you just came to the landing and found him, and the others are in their offices or on the grounds working. Poor man! He fell, and no one was here. But we still have to have the police."

"The ghost did it!" Phoebe declared.

"Ghosts are seldom vicious," Kelsey said.

Phoebe's gaze latched onto Kelsey. "How would you know? Ghosts can be horribly malicious. Ripping off sheets. Throwing coffee pods all around. Oh, you don't know! It was *her*, I'm telling you. She did it!"

Phoebe was pointing. It seemed she was pointing straight at Jane.

"What?" Jane demanded, her voice a squeak rather than the dignified question she'd intended.

But then she saw that they were all looking behind her at the painting on the wall.

She'd noted it before, of course. Just about a month earlier while driving through the area after a situation in the Northeast, she'd seen the castle. It was open three days a week for tours, and she'd been there for the Saturday afternoon event. Mrs. Avery had led the tour and introduced them to Elizabeth Roth via the painting, a young woman who'd lost her fiancé on the eve of their wedding. Elizabeth, the daughter of the house, had been found dead of an overdose of laudanum on the day her wedding should have taken place. It was said that she was often seen in the halls of the castle, wringing her hands as she paced, praying for the return of her lover.

She was beautiful. Rich waves of auburn hair billowed around her face, with soft tendrils curling about her forehead. Her features were fine and delicate and even ethereal. The painting appeared to be that of a ghost, and yet, Mrs. Avery had assured, it had been done from life by the artist Robichaux who'd been a friend of the family. Perhaps he'd sensed the doom that was to be her future. John McCawley, her groom, had been killed the night before the intended nuptials, hunting in the nearby woods.

"Miss Martin, you're suggesting that Elizabeth Roth did this?" Sloan asked quietly.

Phoebe nodded solemnly. "There have been other deaths over the years. On this staircase. Why do you think we're not booked solidly for weddings?"

Sloan looked over at Jane. She stared back at him with her eyes widening. No, she had to admit, she hadn't done much research on the castle. It had just been beautiful and available, perfect for the two of them. Or so she had thought.

A wry half-smile played lightly on Sloan's lips. An assuring smile, she thought. One that conveyed what she already knew. Ghosts don't stay behind to kill. And something else. They both knew they would be together always, whether this turned out to be the wonderful event of a wedding or not.

"Someone else died here? On these steps?" Sloan asked.

Phoebe looked at Jane. "Last time, it was the bride."

Sloan stared at Jane again. She widened her eyes and gave her head a little shake. Another point she had not thought about either.

"What happened?" Logan asked.

"The bride fell. She tumbled down the stairs. The police said that she tripped on her dress and fell. She died in a pool of white. It was terrible!" Phoebe said.

"It doesn't seem to be a particularly dangerous staircase," Kelsey murmured.

Jane looked down again at Marty MacDonald, dead at the foot of the stairs, his eyes still open in horror. As if he'd seen something awful. His murderer? Or something else? Why the hell would anyone have murdered the man? She realized that

Sloan was watching her, frowning, aware of how upset she was. Or maybe relieved? Last time, it had been the bride to die. Sloan gave her a warning look filled with empathy. One that said this was sad, but there was no reason to believe it was anything other than a tragic accident.

"It has to be the ghost. It has to be," Phoebe whispered.

He gave his attention back to Phoebe Martin.

"Must be a powerful ghost," he suggested, not arguing with Phoebe but trying to get her to converse, without really stating anything they knew about the ghost world. "The reverend was not a small man. Assuming that they exist, I'm sure that ghosts do have certain powers. But, personally, I do find it unlikely that the ghost of Elizabeth Roth pushed a man down the stairs."

"You don't know our ghosts," Phoebe said, sounding a little desperate. "Maybe it wasn't Elizabeth. Maybe it was John McCawley, her fiancé. Oh! Maybe his hunting accident wasn't so accidental. Maybe he's seeking revenge!"

There was no painting anywhere of John McCawley, but then, he hadn't lived to become a member of the family and only family members, Mrs. Avery had assured Jane, were pictured on the walls.

"Most likely the poor Reverend MacDonald tripped," Sloan said. "But that's still a sad, accidental death. I believe we should gather everyone on the property here. The police will be arriving soon," Sloan said.

"Of course. I'll gather the others," Phoebe said.

But before she could scamper off, a man in his late-twenties with sandy blond hair, a trifle long, dressed in a tailored shirt and jacket reminiscent of Lord Byron, appeared at the landing.

"What in the devil? What's going on down there?"

Miss Martin didn't scream in terror again. She gaped in astonishment, staring upward.

"Mr. Roth!" she strangled out.

Jane arched her neck to get a better look at the man. Mrs. Avery had informed her that the owner would be gone for the duration of time they were at the castle. He'd supposedly left several weeks ago.

"Hello, Miss Martin," he said gravely.

"Hello," he said to the others, coming down the stairs and carefully avoiding the fallen dead man. He seemed justly appalled by the corpse, sadness, confusion, and horror appearing in his expression as he looked at the dead man.

"Mr. Roth?" Jane asked.

He nodded. "How do you do? Yes, I know. I'm not supposed to be here. And I'm so sorry. Poor man. Do you have any idea... the banister is safe, the carpeting is... secure. I've had engineers in here to make sure that it's safe. But, poor, poor fellow! He must have fallen. Are the police coming?"

"On their way," Kelsey said.

"It's just a normal stairway," Emil Roth murmured, looking up the stairs again. "How does it happen?" The question seemed to be retrospective.

"Mr. Roth, we just heard that a woman died here in the same way. Is that true?" Sloan asked.

Roth nodded, disturbed as he looked down again, then away, as if he couldn't bear to look at the dead man. "Can we do something? Put a sheet on him, something?"

"What about others?" Logan asked. "Dying here."

Roth looked at Logan. "Sir, many died over the years, I believe. It was the Cadawil family home in Wales and the family died out. And here, my parents both died in the room I now keep. Of natural causes. A child in the 1880s died of consumption or tuberculosis. Only Elizabeth Roth died by her own hand. Yes, we had a tragic accident the last time we agreed to have a wedding here. The bride died. A terrible, incredibly sad accident. Oh, Lord. I just wish that we could cover him up!"

"Not until the police arrive," Sloan said. "Best to leave him for the authorities."

Phoebe was still just standing.

"Miss Martin, if you'll gather the others, please?" Logan said gently.

Phoebe moved at last, walking slowly away at first, staring at them all, then turning to run as if banshees were at her heels.

Jane heard the first siren.

She was surprised when Emil Roth looked straight into her eyes. He seemed to study her as if he saw something remarkable.

"How?" he repeated, and then he said, "Why?"

The sound of his voice seemed to echo a sickness within him.

The police arrived. Two officers in uniform preceded a pair of detectives, one grizzled and graying in a tweed coat, the other younger in a stylish jacket. Sloan, closest to the door where they were entering, stepped forward and introduced himself and the others with a minimum of words and explained the situation. A Detective Forester, the older man, asked them all to step away. A younger detective, Flick, began the process of having the uniform officers tape off the scene. Everyone was led through the foyer to the Great Hall. They sat and Jane explained that the minister had been there to officiate at her wedding to Sloan. Emil Roth began to explain that he'd been in Europe planning for an extended stay in Africa but that a stomach bug had soured that prospect, so he'd returned late last night, entering through his private entry at the rear of the castle, where once upon a time guests of the family had arrived via their carriages or on horseback.

The others at the castle were herded into the Grand Hall and introduced themselves. Mrs. Avery, the iron matron in perfect appearance and coiffure. Scully Adair, her young redheaded assistant. Chef Bo Gerard, fortyish and plump, like a man who enjoyed his own creations. Two young cooks, Harry Taubolt and Devon Richard—both lean young men in their twenties who'd not yet enjoyed too much of their own cooking. Sonia Anderson and Lila Adkins, the other maids, young and attractive, like Phoebe.

None of them had been near the foyer, they said.

They were all astounded and saddened by the death of the minister. A few mentioned Cally Thorpe, the young woman who'd died in her bridal gown, tripping down the stairs too. Everyone seemed convinced that it was an accident caused by the ghost of Elizabeth Roth. The medical examiner arrived and while he said he'd have to perform an autopsy, it did appear that the minister had simply missed a step near the second floor landing and tragically broken his neck.

"Sad," Detective Forester said. "Ladies and gentlemen, there will be an autopsy, of course, and I may need to speak to all of you again, but—"

His voice trailed as his younger partner entered from the foyer and whispered something to him. He suddenly studied the four agents.

"You're Feds?" he demanded.

Logan nodded.

"And you're here for a wedding?" Forester asked.

He seemed irritated. But, obviously, they hadn't come to solve any mysteries since they'd been here already when the death had occurred.

"We're here for our wedding," Jane said. "I love the castle. It's beautiful."

"So you're responsible for the minister being here?" Forester asked.

"Yes," she told him.

He stared at her as if it were entirely her fault.

Then Scully Adair, Mrs. Avery's pretty redheaded assistant,

stood up, seemingly anguished. "It's not Miss Everett's fault that this happened. It's the castle's fault. It's true! People can't be married here. It was crazy to think that we could plan a wedding. Something bad was destined to happen."

"Oh, rubbish!" Mrs. Avery protested. "Sit down, Scully. That's rot and foolishness. The poor man had an accident. Miss Everett," she said, looking at Jane. "Not to worry. We can find you another minister."

Jane was appalled by the suggestion. Mrs. Avery made it sound as if a caterer had backed out of making a wedding cake. A man was dead!

"The ghosts did it," Phoebe said.

"Ghosts!" Forester let out a snort of derision and stood. "I believe the medical examiner has taken the body. I have a crime scene unit checking out the stairway, but then there will be hundreds of prints on the banister." He paused and looked around again at all of them. "None of you saw or heard a thing, right?"

"Not until I found him," Phoebe said.

"And then she screamed, and we came running," Sloan said.

Forester nodded. "All right, then, I'll be in touch. We'll be awaiting the M.E.'s report, but I believe we're looking at a tragic accident."

Jane knew what his next words would be.

"None of you leaves town, though. Yeah, I know it's cliché, but that's the way it is. I want to be able to contact each and every one of you easily over the next few days."

He stared at Sloan, Logan, Kelsey, and Jane.

"Especially you Feds."

Chapter Two

For a long moment, Sloan Trent had simply sat beside Jane when the meeting had ended and others, except for Kelsey and Logan, had moved on. Then Sloan had held Jane close in silence. The bond between them remained. Nothing, he thought, could ever break that. And then they sat together with Kelsey and Logan. Maybe they were all still a little numb. They'd come for such a joyous occasion.

"We *can* find a… a…" Kelsey began, but then she paused and Sloan wondered what she had been about to say. *Another minister?* Or, perhaps *a living minister?*

The body of Reverend MacDonald was gone—taken to the morgue. Mrs. Avery had retired to her office. Chef and the cooks had presumably headed to the kitchen. Mr. Green had gone back to the groundskeeper's lodge and the maids were cleaning the rooms above.

"I'm not sure that this is what we want for the memory anymore," Sloan said, slipping his arm around Jane's shoulder. She was handling it well, he thought.

Or maybe not.

She seemed stricken. But Jane was strong. She'd proven that so many times. Of course, this was different. She'd planned the perfect small wedding for them in a beautiful place with just a few close friends. The ceremony had never meant that much to him. If she'd wanted a big wedding, fine. If she'd wanted to walk into city hall and say a few words, that would have been fine, too.

He knew that he loved her. No, that was truly a mild concept for the way he felt about her. He'd known what people might refer to as "the good, the bad, and the ugly" in life. He'd experienced a few one-night stands, never knowing if they were good women or not. He'd had relationships with really fine people. But he'd never been with anyone like Jane. Smart, funny, beautiful. And she'd be just as beautiful to him in fifty years. She had the most unusual eyes, not brown or hazel, more a true amber. When she looked at him with those eyes, he saw the world and everything he wanted in life within them. The idea that someone else completed him as a whole seemed cliché, and yet he woke each day happy she was in his life. He worked well with her. They trusted one another with no question. Their commitment was complete. And it didn't matter to him a bit if it was legal. But since they did both believe in God, along with the basic tenets of goodness associated with most religions, it was nice to think that they'd have their union blessed.

Where or how meant nothing to him.

But women? They planned weddings. Big and small.

"We're not getting another minister," Jane said. "And we're not getting married here."

"But we're not leaving here, you know. Especially not us 'Feds,'" Logan reminded them.

Sloan was glad to see that Logan was amused rather than offended. Most of the time when they worked with locals, all went well. Sloan knew that because once upon a time he'd been the local the Krewe of Hunters—with Logan at the helm—had worked with. That had been the beginning for him. Now, he'd been with the Krewe for some time and he loved where he was, though he didn't particularly like murder and mayhem. But he'd known as a young man he'd been meant to fight for the rights of victims, whether living or dead. And working with the Krewe was the best way he knew how to accomplish that role.

Jane punched Logan in the arm.

The two had known each other for years. Logan had been a Texas Ranger. Sloan had spent time working in Texas, too, but Jane had been a civilian forensic artist who'd worked with Logan's group many times before any of them had ever heard of the Krewe of Hunters. They sometimes seemed like a brother and sister act.

"No matter what Detective Forester said, we all know damned well we're not leaving. Not until we know what happened to our minister," Jane said.

"It was an accident, don't you know?" Kelsey said. "That, or the ghost did it."

"We've yet to come across a malevolent ghost," Logan reminded Kelsey.

"And I don't believe for one minute that a ghost did anything," Kelsey said. She looked at Jane. "Have you seen any of the ghosts that haunt the place?"

Jane shook her head. "I didn't see any signs of anyone haunting the castle when I was here before, nor have I seen any yet. How about you?"

Kelsey shook her head. "But you and Sloan arrived much earlier. I thought that maybe while you were out in the garden, or over by the old graveyard, you might have seen someone."

"We're forgetting one thing," Logan said.

"What's that?" Jane asked.

"We're suspicious people by nature. We're called in to solve unexplained deaths, attacks, and other events. And this might have been accidental," Logan said. "Maybe Reverend MacDonald just wasn't paying attention. Don't forget, we never suspect anything but what is real and solid until we've given up on real and solid."

"Then again," Sloan pointed out, "if we're not suspicious, I don't think anyone else will be. Because it *appears* to be real and solid that our minister tripped and broke his neck tumbling down the stairs." He stroked Jane's dark hair and looked into her luminous eyes. "You met the Reverend MacDonald in the village, right?"

She nodded. "When I came here and saw the castle on the hill, I thought it was just perfect. I had gone into a coffee shop and the clerk there told me that it was open for tours. After I spoke to Mrs. Avery and discovered we could get this date, I went back down to the village and inquired about someone at the library. I met with Reverend MacDonald in the same coffee shop and he was delighted. He couldn't marry us on a Sunday because of his church services, but a Saturday would be marvelous. And I told him I'd have a room for him here, so that he'd be ready for the services."

"What else do you know about him?" Sloan asked her.

"Nothing, except that he's from the area. A bachelor. He loves when his youth groups have cookie sales. And the parents he works with are wonderful and love to work at creating carnivals to support the church."

"Doesn't sound like a man anyone would want to hurt," Logan said.

"No," Kelsey agreed.

"He looks great on the surface," Sloan murmured. He caught Logan's eye and he knew. What had happened might have been a tragic accident. But, they wouldn't just accept that as fact. They'd dig and see what might lie hidden beneath appearances.

"Okay, then," Kelsey said. "I'm up and off."

"Off where?" Jane asked her.

"To the local library. I'll see what I can dig up about this place," Kelsey said. "And then I'll head to the church and speak with people and find out what I can about our good Reverend MacDonald."

"Then I'm... not really off," Jane said. "I'm going to talk

to Scully Adair. Bad things have happened here before. We need to find out more about the bride who died."

"I'll head into the village, too," Logan said. "And see what I can dig up by way of gossip there regarding both the reverend and the castle folk. I think I saw Mr. Emil Roth head out. It would be good to have a chat with him. The castle's hereditary owner should definitely know what there is to know about the castle."

"We'll meet back upstairs in a couple of hours?" Jane asked. "In the bridal suite? It's the biggest and gives us the most room to work."

"We might as well make use of the size," Sloan agreed dryly.

They wouldn't be laughing tonight, sipping champagne, eating strawberries and enjoying a totally carefree time as their first night of being husband and wife.

"You know, maybe you two are not going to become legally wed here," Kelsey pointed out, a smile in her eyes, "but there's no reason to make a perfectly good room go to waste."

"Don't worry," Sloan told her, smiling and meeting Jane's eyes. "We don't intend for you two to stay long."

"A man just died," Jane murmured.

"In our line of work, someone has frequently just died," Logan said softly. "And that really shows us just how important it is to *live*."

Jane smiled and nodded. "We have champagne and fruit and chocolate. And we're willing to share. We'll meet in the suite in about two hours. And we will know the truth."

Sloan looked at Jane as they all nodded. She was so beautiful. Calmer where Kelsey could be animated, serene often in a way that seemed to make the world stand still and be all right for him. She could be passionate and filled with vehemence when she chose and courageous at all times—even when she was afraid.

God, he loved her.

* * * *

Scully Adair's place was the reception desk in front of the doors that led to Mrs. Avery's medieval and elegant office on the ground floor of the castle. Mrs. Avery, Jane thought, was going to be a tough nut to crack. She was all business and no nonsense. But, of course, if she heard Jane talking with Scully, she'd probably butt right in. So Jane waited, standing by the office door. Soon enough, Scully came out, her pretty features furrowed in a frown, her movements indicating that she was disturbed and restless. Her fingers fluttered as she closed the office door. There was a twitch in her cheek.

"Hey," Jane said softly.

She was glad that Scully didn't scream in surprise. Instead, her slender fingers flitted to her face. Her hand rested at her throat.

"Um, hey," she said. "I'm so, so sorry. I mean, what a wedding day, huh?"

"I'm not worried about my wedding," Jane said. "Sloan and I will marry somewhere soon enough. But were you going for lunch or a cup of coffee?"

Scully nodded with wide eyes. "Coffee, with a stiff shot."

"May I go with you?" Jane asked.

"Sure. I guess."

Jane fell into step with her as they walked along a corridor to the far end of the ground floor. There, an archway led into a cavernous kitchen. Pots and pans hung from rafters. A giant fireplace and hearth filled one end. Other than that, the place was state of the art with giant refrigerators and freezers, a range top surrounded by granite, a work table, and other modern appliances. There was also a large table in a breakfast nook. Old paned windows looked out over the cliff top where flowers and shrubs grew in beautiful profusion.

Chef Bo Gerard, a man who greatly resembled Chef Boyardee, and his two young assistants, Harry Taubolt—dark-haired and lean, a handsome young man in his mid-twenties—and Devon Richard, blond, a little heavier, a little older, and bearing the marks of teenage acne—were already there. They all looked morose. Each had a mug in front of him as if they were all imbibing in coffee, but a large bottle of Jameson's sat in the middle of the table between them. The three looked up from their cups and smiled grimly at seeing Scully, then leapt to their feet when they saw Jane.

"Miss, guests aren't really allowed back here," Chef Gerard said.

"Oh, leave her be. What, does she look stupid? They're going to look up everything about this place," Scully said. She walked past the table, heading toward the granite counter and a coffee pot. "Miss Everett, coffee? You can lace it or not as you choose. The guys already have the booze on the table. Me? My minister dead on my wedding day? I'd be drinking."

Jane smiled. "Coffee, yes, lovely, thank you."

She accepted a cup from Scully, who sat and poured herself a liberal amount of Jameson's from the bottle on the table.

Not about to let an uncomfortable silence begin, Jane dove right in. "Scully, you said that we shouldn't have been allowed to plan a wedding here. Why? What happened before."

"Scully!" Chef said.

Scully stared at him and then looked at Jane. "You know the legend, of course. I was so startled and so scared when I saw the poor Reverend MacDonald. I looked at *her* picture. I mean, seriously, who knows? Maybe she can push people down the stairs."

"Scully, you're an idiot," Harry Taubolt said, shaking his dark head. "You see ghosts everywhere."

"There are ghosts," Devon Richard said, staring into his cup. He looked at Jane then as if she had somehow willed him to do so. "There are ghosts. They can move things."

Chef let out an impatient sound. Harry snorted.

"You forget where you put things or what you've done, that's what happens," Chef said.

"No," Devon said, shaking his head firmly. "When I come out to the Great Hall and find a napkin on the floor, I know I didn't put it there. When I've preset a plate with garnish, then the garnish is on the counter top, I know I didn't put it there." He turned to stare at Harry. "And you know it happens. You just have to deny it, or you'd be scared."

"You think that Elizabeth Roth is the ghost?" Jane asked.

"No," Scully said.

"Yes!" Chef snapped firmly.

"An old ghost," Harry said softly. "Elizabeth was due to marry John McCawley just before the start of the Civil War. McCawley was from the South. He wasn't in the military, he hadn't made any declarations about secession, but the family wasn't happy about the marriage. I say one of them did McCawley in when he was out in the woods. Hunting accident? Hell, no one believes that. Nathaniel Roth, Elizabeth's brother, was out in the woods at the same time. He must have shot McCawley. And Elizabeth couldn't bear it or the fact that her family would be party to such a thing. She killed herself—that we know. And she hates the family. She couldn't be married here, so she won't let anyone else be married here. She pushed your minister down the stairs."

"She looked beautiful and gentle, not like a vengeful murderess," Jane said. She turned quickly to Scully. "Who do you think is haunting the place?"

"Scully," Chef said.

But Scully laughed. "Jane is an FBI agent. You think she can't find out?" Scully told Jane, "Mrs. Avery decided three years ago that she'd allow a man and woman from Georgia to be married here. Cally Thorpe was going to marry Fred Grigsby. Cally fell down the stairs, too. Detective Forester didn't mention that fact because he was working somewhere else when it happened. He'll know now, but, anyway, what the hell? That was ruled an accident, too."

"So," Jane said carefully, "you think that Cally was pushed?"

"How many people really just fall down the stairs?" Scully demanded and shivered. "I think I have to quit. I mean, I love this place, but we were alright before Mrs. Avery booked another wedding. What is the matter with that woman?"

"How many of the people working here today were working here when Cally Thorpe died?" Jane asked.

They looked around the table at one another.

"Let's see," Chef began. "Harry, you had just started. Devon, you'd been here a month or so. Mrs. Avery, of course, and Mr. Green has been here since he was a kid working with his dad on the property. Me, of course. I've been here eight years."

"What about the maids?" Jane asked.

"Just Phoebe. The other two girls started in the last few years," Scully said. "I've been here for five… oh, God! I was the one who found Cally. Her eyes were open, too. She was just staring toward the ceiling. No. It wasn't the ceiling. It was the painting." She leaned forward, focusing on Jane. "She was staring at the painting of Elizabeth Roth, right there, right where it hung on the wall."

"Maybe it's true," Devon said quietly. "Maybe we're all okay as long as no one gets married here. Maybe Elizabeth has remained all these years—and she'll kill someone before she allows a wedding to take place in this house!"

Chapter Three

Sloan had feared he might have some trouble with Emil Roth. After all, he was liable for what had happened, being the castle's owner. Even if lawyers could argue that the man wasn't responsible for another's accident on a safe stairway, he was liable in his own mind.

That had to hurt.

Sloan had seen him head out the front with the police when they'd left, and he hadn't seen him since, so he decided to take a walk outside first and see if he was down by the gates or perhaps just sitting on one of the benches in the gardens. While the castle was on a cliff and surrounded on three sides by bracken and flowers, beautifully wild, the front offered sculptures and rock gardens and trails through flowers and bushes and even a manicured hedge menagerie. Mr. Green apparently worked hard and certainly earned his keep. But Sloan couldn't find Emil Roth outside. He tapped on the caretaker's door and Mr. Green opened it to him, looking at him suspiciously.

"Yeah? You got a problem here? You gotta bring it up with management," Green said.

"No, sir. No problem. It's beautiful. I've never seen such a perfectly manicured lawn. Yet you keep the wild and windswept and exotic look around the place, too," Sloan said. "I was just looking for Mr. Roth."

"He ain't out here," Green said. He was an older, grizzled man, lean yet strong, his skin weathered and permanently tanned from years in the sun.

"Then, thank you. And, sincerely, my compliments. You keep this up all alone?"

"Two kids come to mow and hedge sometimes, but... yeah, I do most of it," Green said.

Sloan thought he might have seen a blush rise to the man's cheeks.

"I've been doing this since I was a kid, over fifty years now. The old Emil—this Emil's father—hell, everyone was named Emil in the darned family—just opened the place to the public about forty years ago. My dad was still in charge and he taught me. People like greenery. It's a concrete world, you know? Some people come just to see the grounds."

"I can imagine. Hey, so how has it been for you? What do you think? I mean, the castle goes way back, but even in the United States, it has a spooky history. The obligatory ghost," Sloan said.

Green narrowed his eyes. "Sure. All old places have ghosts."

"You've seen something," Sloan said.

"Naw."

"I can tell!"

"Sane people scoff at ghosts, you know."

"Only sane people who haven't seen them yet," Sloan said.

"Have you seen a ghost?"

"One or two, I'm pretty damned sure," Sloan said. "You gotta be careful—because people don't think you're sane once you mention the unusual."

Green nodded in complete, conspiratorial agreement. He lowered his voice, despite the fact that they were alone with no one remotely near them.

"There are ghosts around here. A couple of them.

There's—" He hesitated, as if still not sure, but Sloan stayed silent, watching him, waiting. "—a man in boots and breeches and a black shirt who watches me sometimes. He tends to stay behind the trees, down toward what's left of the forest to the rear of the property. And as far as Elizabeth Roth goes, I've seen her. I've seen her often, from the upstairs window. Her room—Elizabeth's room—it's the bridal suite now. I guess you're staying in it."

Sloan nodded. "That's us. I'll watch out for Elizabeth," he said. "Tell me, has anything ever indicated to you that the ghosts could be—mean? Vindictive?"

Green shook his head. "Naw, in fact... hell, one day I slipped on some wet grass and went tumbling down. It was summer and I blacked out. When I woke up, all dizzy and parched, a water bottle came rolling down to me. Now sure, bottles can roll. But I think John McCawley was there. He rolled that bottle to me. I took a drink, got myself up, and all was well. There's nothing mean about the ghosts in this place."

"You were here when another accident took place, right?"

Again, Green nodded. "Poor thing. That girl broke her neck on the stairs, same as the minister today. We checked the banister. The carpeting on the stairs is checked constantly to see that it's not ripped. The stairs aren't particularly steep or winding. Go figure. Bad things happen."

Sloan thanked Green and headed back toward the house. The foyer and Great Hall were empty. He heard voices coming from the kitchen but headed toward the stairs. At the top, he could see one of the maids.

Phoebe Martin.

She seemed to still be in shock and was stroking a polish rag over the same piece of banister over and over.

Sloan walked up the stairs. "You doing okay?" he asked.

"It's just so sad. How about you?"

"We're all right. Did you know Reverend MacDonald?"

"No, I'm bad, I guess. I haven't gone to church in years. And I was raised Catholic. I wouldn't have known Reverend MacDonald anyway. He was at the really small parish just outside town, and he was an Episcopalian, I believe."

"You never saw him around town?"

Phoebe shook her head. "No, I guess we didn't shop at the same places. And, I admit, I'm pretty into clubbing. Not many ministers go clubbing, I guess."

"Ah, well. I was hoping to talk to Mr. Roth."

Phoebe's eyes widened. "Can you believe it? He was here when this happened, and he wasn't supposed to be."

"Since he is here, I was hoping to talk with him."

"That's his suite, there, at the end of the hall." She lowered her voice. "That was always the room that was kept for the master of the house. And there has been a Roth here since the castle was brought to the United States." She hesitated. "You know, don't you, that the bridal suite was once Elizabeth Roth's room when she was alive?"

"I've been told."

Phoebe looked at him with wide, worried eyes. "You need to be careful. Especially careful now."

"I don't believe Elizabeth would want to hurt Jane or me."

"She hurt the Reverend MacDonald," Phoebe said. "I truly believe it."

"Phoebe, sadly, accidents do happen."

"They happen more often with ghosts," she insisted.

"What does Mr. Roth believe about the place, or do you know?" Sloan asked.

"He doesn't believe in ghosts. Which is good—I guess. But then, he's not here a lot. Too quiet for Mr. Roth. He likes Boston and New York and travel in general. I guess if I had his money, I'd travel, too."

"Everyone can travel some," Sloan told her.

"Sure," Phoebe said. "But, still... be careful, please."

"We'll do that. I promise," Sloan told her. "And perhaps, if you're worried, you might not want to work on the banister."

"Oh. *Oh!*" Phoebe said. "Right!" Gripping the banister tightly, she started down the stairs.

Sloan smiled, thanked her, and headed down the hall. He knocked at the double French doors that led to the suite. Emil Roth answered so quickly that he wondered if he'd been waiting for a summons.

"What can I do for you?" Roth asked.

Sloan studied the man. He was young to have such financial power, Sloan thought. Late-twenties, tops. And he seemed to enjoy the look of a Renaissance poet. His haircut would make him perfect for a Shakespearean play. But his gaze was steady as he looked at Sloan.

"Since you're here, I was hoping you'd give me a tour of the castle and a tour of your family history," Sloan said.

Roth stared at him. He was a man with a medium build and light eyes that added to what was almost a fragile-poet look.

"Sometimes, family history sucks, you know?" he said. "I'm sorry about your wedding. I mean, really sorry that a man is dead. By all accounts a good and jovial man. And I'm sorry that my family history is full of asses. But I don't think that it means anything. A man fell. That's it. He died. So tragic."

"I agree. But, we're not getting married today and we're still here. And history fascinates me," Sloan told him.

Roth grinned at that. "You're a Fed involved with a special unit that investigates when deaths that are rumored to be associated with something paranormal happen. I'm young, rich, and not particularly responsible, but I'm not stupid either."

Sloan laughed. "I wouldn't begin to suggest that you're stupid. I believe that, tragically, Reverend MacDonald fell. But I am fascinated with this place. Jane didn't really check out much of the history here. She fell in love with the castle. She wanted a small and intimate wedding more or less on the spur of the moment. And sure, under the circumstances, I'd love to know more about the 'ghosts' that supposedly reside here."

Roth grimaced. "The maids have been talking again."

"Everyone talks. Ghost stories are fun."

"So I hear. Mrs. Avery thinks that they create the mystique of the castle. I personally think that my ancestor's desire to bring a castle to the United States is interesting enough. But, we do keep up a lot of the maintenance with our bed and breakfast income, parties, and tours. So, I let her go on about the brilliance of a good ghost story. But, what the hell? I'll give you a tour."

"That's great. I really appreciate it," Sloan told him.

"What about your fiancée? Maybe she'd like to come, too?" Roth suggested.

"Maybe she would. I'm not sure where she is… I'll try her cell," Sloan said.

Jane was number one on his speed dial and, in a matter of seconds, she answered. He cheerfully explained where he was and asked what she was doing. She said that she'd be right there.

As they waited, Roth asked Sloan, "How do you like your room? No ghostly disturbances, right?"

"Not a one," Sloan told him.

"You should see people around here when they come for the ghost tours," Roth said. "They all have their cameras out like eager puppies. They catch dust specs that become 'orbs.' Sad. But, then again, we're featured in a lot of books and again, I guess my dear Mrs. Avery is right."

"I understand she's a distant relative," Sloan said. "Pardon me for overstepping, but it doesn't sound as if you like her much."

Roth grinned. "I'm that transparent? Sad. No, I don't like

her. Her grandmother was my grandfather's sister. I guess we're second cousins or something like that. But, no, I don't like her. She's self-righteous and knows everything. I understand keeping the place up and keeping it maintained, but she's turned it into a theme attraction. I'm really proud of it as a family home. But... anyway, in my father's will he asked that I keep her employed through her lifetime—as long as she wishes. So, there you go. She's no spring chicken, but she's a pretty healthy sixty-plus. I have a few years to go."

Sloan heard footsteps in the hall and saw Jane coming.

They always managed a real balance when working, as did the others. Those in the Krewe of Hunters units tended to pair up—maybe there was just something special that they all shared and that created a special attraction. Jane had belonged to the Krewe before he had. He'd met her when she'd come to Lily, Arizona, his home, where he'd returned when his grandfather had suffered from cancer. She'd been both amazing and annoying to him from first sight. He'd been attracted to her from the start, falling in love with her smile, her eyes, her mind. In his life, he'd never been with anyone like her. She seemed aware of everything about him, faults and flaws and "talents," and she loved him. They hadn't been in a hurry to get married, but they'd both wanted it.

She met his eyes with the same open gaze she always did.

He walked to meet her, slipping his arm around her shoulder. "I'm really pleased. It's not a good day, certainly, but Emil Roth has offered us a real tour. History, and all else."

"That's kind of you, Mr. Roth," Jane said.

"But you saw the castle before, right? You took the ghost tour, didn't you?" Roth asked her.

"I took the tour. So I know about Elizabeth Roth and her beloved, John McCawley. He was killed in a hunting accident the day before the wedding, and then Elizabeth killed herself."

"Come on then. I do give the best tour," Roth said. "And

call me Emil, please."

"Then we're Sloan and Jane," Sloan said.

Emil smiled and nodded. "Let's start in the Great Hall and go from there."

He seemed happy. Sloan looked at Jane. He took her hand and she smiled and shrugged and they followed Emil Roth. At the Great Hall, he extended his hands, as if displaying the massive room with its décor of swords and coats of arms and standing men in armor.

"Castle Cadawil was built in 1280 and the Duke of Cadawil held it all of two years, until the death of Llywelyn the Last in 1282 and the conquest of Edward I from the Principality of Wales. That's why, to this day, the heir apparent to the British crown is called the Prince of Wales. Anyway, the castle wasn't a major holding. It was on a bluff with nothing around it that anyone really wanted to hold for any reason. So, through the centuries, it had been abandoned, half-restored, abandoned again. In the early 1800s, my self-made millionaire ancestor saw it there and determined that he could move a castle to New England. And he did so. Of course, when it came over, it was little but design and stone. Antiques were purchased and through the years, Tiffany windows added. My family apparently loved their castle. But then, as you know, tragedy struck before the wedding of Elizabeth Roth and John McCawley."

"What do you think about that?" Jane asked him. "Did the family love and welcome McCawley, or did someone hate him?"

"Enough to kill him?" Roth asked.

"He died in a hunting accident. Other men in the family were out there, too, right?" Jane asked.

"Yes, they were. And it's an interesting question. There are no letters or family records that reflect anyone's feelings on the matter and the two men involved would have been my great,

great, great, grandfather, Emil Roth, and my great, great, grandfather, another Emil Roth. I don't like to think that my ancestors would have killed a man they didn't want marrying into the family."

"What happened?" Sloan asked. "McCawley was shot?"

"With an arrow, they were deer hunting," Roth said. "But, you see, they weren't the only ones out there. A number of wedding guests were there. You two wanted a small wedding. The wedding of Elizabeth Roth was the social event of the season."

"Of course," Jane said.

"No one saw anything? No one knew who missed a deer and killed a man?" Sloan asked.

"If so, no one admitted anything. He was found by Elizabeth's father who, of course, immediately rushed him back to the castle and called for a surgeon. But it was too late. Elizabeth came running down the stairs and—"

Roth paused in his speaking, looking troubled.

"And?"

"The story goes that John McCawley died at the foot of the stairs. The men carrying him paused there because Elizabeth was rushing down. When she reached him, he looked into her eyes, closed his own, and died."

"How sad," Jane murmured.

"And then, of course, that night, Elizabeth took an overdose of laudanum and died in the early hours of the following morning, when the wedding should have taken place."

He led them out of the hall.

"If you look at the arches, you can see that the foyer was originally a last defense before the actual castle. There would have been a keep, of course, in Wales, and a wall surrounding it. We have the lawn in front and the wild growth to the rear, except for where the grass is mown just out the back.

Following along to the right of the castle, after the entry, you reach the offices and such and going all the way back, you get to the kitchen. Heading upstairs, are the rooms. Mine, of course, was always the master's suite. Where you're sleeping— and though they weren't actually married here, many a bride and groom have slept there—was Elizabeth's room. There are four more bedrooms. Your friends are in one. Reverend MacDonald was in another, and there are two more guest rooms. The attic holds five rooms. Phoebe lives in one and the other two maids come in just for the day or special occasions. Chef has an apartment over the old stables, and Mr. Green has an apartment on the property, too."

"Mrs. Avery doesn't live here?" Jane asked.

"Yes, she's on the property. You passed her place coming in. The old guard house at the foot of the cliff. But her assistant, Scully, lives in the village as do the other cooks."

He looked at Jane curiously.

She asked him, "Is there a big black spot on my face that no one is mentioning to me?"

Emil Roth laughed. "I beg your pardon. Forgive me. It's just that when I look at you and your face, tilted at a certain angle, you look so much like her."

"Her?" Jane asked.

"Elizabeth," Emil said. "Come look at the painting again."

Sloan wasn't sure why the idea disturbed him but he followed as they headed to look at the painting on the wall. Elizabeth Roth was depicted with her hair piled high atop her head, burnished auburn tendrils trailing around her face. Her eyes appeared hazel at first but when Sloan came closer, he realized they'd been painted a true amber.

Just like Jane's.

There was something in the angle of the features. It was true. Jane bore a resemblance to the woman who'd lived more than a century before her birth.

"Do you have roots up here? Maybe you're a long lost cousin," Emil teased.

Jane shook her head. "My family members were in Texas back when people were exclaiming 'Remember the Alamo!' I've no relatives in this region. It's just a fluke."

"But an interesting one," Roth said. "So, what would you like to see next?"

"Where is Elizabeth buried?" Sloan asked. "And, for that matter, her fiancé, John McCawley."

"I understand he never actually became family so he has no painting in the castle," Jane said. "But surely they buried the poor fellow."

"Absolutely. Out to the rear, at the rise to the highest cliff. They're both in the chapel."

"I think I'd like to pay them tribute," Jane said.

"If you wish," Roth said. Smiling, he turned to lead the way out of the castle. "Although, I will warn you."

"What's that?" Sloan asked.

"On a day like today, with a fog settling over the graves, people have been known to see ghosts wandering about."

Sloan looked at Jane. "That's okay. We'll take our chances."

Chapter Four

The old chapel had been brought over to the States from Wales, Roth explained as they left via the rear, out through the kitchen's delivery doors.

Jane was curious that he had chosen to leave by this route. If she remembered right, there were other exits, more elegantly designed, leading to the wilds of the rear and the cliffs that overlooked the sea.

Chef and his two cooks were no longer sitting at the table imbibing in coffee and Jameson's, she noted as they went through. They were all busy at some kind of prep work. She assumed that the employees ate dinner at the castle as well since they didn't need that much prep for four guests and the master of the house, who they hadn't expected to be there anyway.

Chef Bo looked up from his work at a saucepan and acknowledged Roth and stared broodingly at the others as they went through.

His two assistants just watched.

"There's another way out as well. The two arches at the end of the Great Hall lead to smaller halls that bypass this area," Roth explained. "And there's a servants stairway back there, too. I just thought it would be fun to see what was going on in the kitchen."

He was almost like a child who knew that he was in charge,

and was yet surprised by it and curious as to his effect on others.

"Smells divine!" he called as they passed.

Three "thank yous" followed his words.

There was a large doorway under a sheltered porte-cochère when they stepped outside. Most likely, parking for large delivery trucks. They walked around one of the walls and were in the back. An open-air patio, set on stone, offered amazing views of the Atlantic Ocean. A light fog swirled in a breeze and seemed in magical motion, barely there. A fireplace, stocked with dry logs, remained ready for those who came out to enjoy the view when it was cool, and Jane imagined they might hold barbecues out there too. Bracken grew around the patio with wild flowers in beautiful colors. Other than the patio and the chairs, if one stood on the cliff and looked out or up at the rise of the castle walls, they might have been in a distant land and in a different time.

But Jane looked to her right.

At the base of a little cliff that rose to another wild and jagged height, was the chapel. It was surrounded by a low stone wall. Within the wall were numerous graves and plots. The chapel had been built in the Norman style with great rising A-line arches and a medieval design. Two giant gargoyles sat over the double wooden doors that led inside.

"Sometimes," Roth said, "I do feel just a bit like a medieval lord. Pity it's far too small and dangerous here for a joust."

"It's really lovely," Jane said.

"Yes, and I'm a lucky man," Roth said. "Primogeniture and all. The oldest son gets everything. Of course, in my case, I was the only child. If I do have children, I'll change things, that's for sure."

Somewhat surprised, Jane looked at Sloan.

Was that for real? If so, he seemed like a pretty decent guy.

She smiled.

There was that wonderful part of their relationship that seemed like an added boon. The ability to look at one another and know that they shared a thought.

"Shall we head toward the chapel?" Roth asked.

He stood a bit down on a slant from them. He wasn't really that small a man, probably about six feet even. But Sloan seemed to tower over him. Jane was five-nine and in flats, but with his Renaissance-poet look, Roth somehow seemed delicate and fragile.

"Thanks. We'd love to see it," Sloan said.

They followed him to the stone wall. There was a gate in the center and a path that led to the chapel. The gate wasn't locked. It swung in easily at Roth's touch and they followed him. He kept on the stone path and headed directly to the chapel where the door was also unlocked.

"You're not worried about break-ins of any kind?" Sloan asked him.

"Maybe I should be. I guess people do destroy things sometimes just for fun. But Mr. Green is always at his place. He hears anything that goes on. He only looks old. Trust me, he's deceptively spry. Caught me by the ears a few times when I was a kid. Guests here are welcome to use the chapel and the only way up here is by the road, so I guess it was just never kept locked. Progress, though. Maybe I'll have to in the future. It's really kind of a cool place. You'll see. Simple and nice."

It was indeed. Tiffany windows displayed the fourteen Stations of the Cross along the side walls, each with its own recessed altar. The high arches were clean and simple and there were five small pews set before the main altar. A large marble cross rose behind the altar.

"Actually, there's a time capsule in here," Roth told him. "Emil, who brought the castle over, is under the main altar with his wife. Their children are scattered along the sides. Sometimes, of course, the daughters moved away, but there are a good fifty people buried or entombed just in the chapel. But you want our own Roth family Romeo and Juliet. Over there—first altar. Come on."

His footsteps made a strange sound as he hurried along the stone floor. Sloan and Jane followed. There were six altar niches along each side of the structure. Someone had obviously been a stickler for symmetry. The first, closest to the main altar, had a window that depicted Judas's betrayal of Christ. The altar beneath it was adorned with a large silver cross. On exact angles from the prayer bench below the altar were two marble sarcophagi or tombs. One was etched simply with a name. John McCawley. The other bore just a first name. Elizabeth. Beneath her name was a tribute. *Daughter; the rose of our lives, plucked far too swift, and we left in life, adrift. In Spring she lived, in Spring she remains. There 'til our own sweet release, 'til this life on earth for all shall cease. Beloved child, we'll meet again, where sorrows end and souls remain.*

"It sounds as if she was deeply mourned," Jane said.

"They say that her father was never the same. He lived as if he'd welcome death every day."

"It's amazing he didn't fall apart completely and lose everything. But, then, of course, she had a brother. Your great-great-great—however many greats—grandfather," Sloan said.

Emil laughed. "It was my great, great, great grandfather. And he apparently had a wonderful friend as an overseer who'd studied at Harvard. He kept the place going. So this is it. What else can I show you? I mean, you're guests. You're free to wander as you choose. And, of course, this was horribly tragic, but you were supposed to be married today. We'll do anything we can. If you want—"

"We're just fine," Jane said quickly. "Will you be joining us at dinner?"

Roth seemed pleased, as if she were giving him an invitation rather than asking a question.

"I'd be delighted. Much better than eating alone," he said.

"Chef seems busy. Don't others eat here as well?" Jane asked.

"They do. But when I'm here, I just wind up eating in my room," he told him. "And, actually, I have some e-mails to answer. Anything else, just knock on my door."

"We'll wander here for a minute, if it's all right," Sloan told him.

"My house is your house," Roth told them with a grin.

He left them.

When he was gone, Jane looked at Sloan and asked, "Anything?"

"Quiet as—a tomb. No pun intended, of course."

She grimaced at him and headed to the grave of Elizabeth Roth. She set her hand on the tomb, trying to feel something of the young woman who had lived such a short and tragic life. But all she felt was cold stone.

Sloan watched her.

She shrugged. "Nothing. But I can't help but feel that somehow, what's happened now, with Cally Thorpe and Reverend MacDonald, has something to do with the past."

"You really think it's possible that a ghost pushed them both down the stairs?" Sloan asked her, frowning.

"It's not something that we've ever seen. So, no, I don't. But I can't shake the feeling that it's all related."

"Why?" Sloan asked.

She smiled. "I guess that's what we have to figure out."

"Let's walk to the room," Sloan said. "Maybe Kelsey and Logan are back and have come up with something." He reached out and took her hand. "I love you."

She nodded. "I'm not worried about our lives. I'm just sorry that Marty MacDonald is dead."

"If we can stop something from happening in the future, at least he won't have died in vain."

"Let's head up," she said.

* * * *

"There's no dirt to be found on the Reverend MacDonald," Kelsey announced. "His church is being draped in mourning, his deacon has sent for an emergency cover priest to take care of Sunday services. There are no allegations of his ever being flirtatious, too close to the children, or involved in any kind of scandal. But we have more reason to think it was just an accident."

"Oh?" Sloan said.

He was always amazed by the Krewe's ability to find whatever was needed to make their work go smoothly.

The bridal suite—Elizabeth Roth's room—actually consisted of a drawing room or outer area, the bedroom itself, two large dressing rooms, and these days, a small kitchenette area. Kelsey had managed to get hold of a work board. With erasable markers, she'd already started lists of what they knew and what they had learned. Staring at lists sometimes showed them what went with some other piece of information in another column. They were gathered in the drawing room, Sloan and Jane curled on the loveseat together, Kelsey at her board, and Logan thoughtful as he straddled a chair and looked at the board.

"Why should we be more prone to think that it was an accident?" Sloan asked.

"I spoke with the reverend's deacon. He's been battling a heart condition for a long time. It's possible he suffered a minor heart attack and fell," Kelsey said.

"Maybe the M.E. will be able to tell us more from the autopsy. Anything from your end, Logan?" Sloan asked.

"The reverend was well liked. No hint of improprieties or anything along that line," Logan said. "People were sad. But

many of his friends did think he was a walking time bomb. Apparently, a lot of people knew about his condition. And he liked pastries. A woman in the bakery told me that she'd designed a whole line of sugar-free desserts to help him keep his weight down."

"Okay. No one out to get the reverend." Kelsey wrote on the board.

"Both Elizabeth and John McCawley are entombed in the chapel," Jane volunteered. "Along with the rest of the family."

"The caretaker, Mr. Green, sees the ghosts all the time," Sloan said.

"But I don't believe a ghost is doing this," Jane said flatly. "From what I've heard, both Elizabeth and John McCawley were good people—deeply in love. I do, however, have a suspicion that John's death wasn't accidental."

They were all silent.

Kelsey frowned and looked at Sloan.

Sloan spoke to Jane at last. "I don't know if we'll ever have an answer to that. Even if we were to meet their ghosts, they might not have known themselves. What we need to figure out is if someone is killing people here now, in the present, and stop them from killing anyone else."

"Of course," Jane said. She rose, stretched, and walked over to the board. "Personally, I find our young host to be interesting."

"You think that Emil Roth pushed the reverend down the stairs?" Kelsey asked.

"No, and I'm not sure why not. Except that he doesn't seem to be into a lot of family rot. He doesn't see himself as some kind of a lord of the castle. He's young and rich and spoiled, and I think he knows it. I'm not even sure that he likes the castle. He definitely doesn't like Mrs. Avery. He has to keep her here, though. It was part of his father's will. She's a distant relative."

"Ah, the plot thickens," Logan said dryly. "But why would she kill people?"

"To keep the ghost legend going? Maybe she wants some of the television ghost hunters to come in here. Great publicity for the place," Jane suggested.

"Logan," Sloan said, "let's call the home office and get someone there checking into financials for this place. As far as I can tell, the Roth family has more than Emil could spend in a lifetime, even if he tried wasting every cent of it."

"There's no reason for the man to have killed a minister," Kelsey said.

"Or anyone, really," Sloan noted. "But, we'll get a financial check done on the family and make sure. So, anyone get any dirt on the people living here?"

"Not yet. Observation may help," Sloan said. "We'll be dining with the master of the house, and I believe dinner is at six."

"Ah, yes, the wedding feast." Jane murmured.

"We can still—" Sloan began.

"No, we can't!" Jane said quickly. "The wedding feast will be fine, without the wedding."

"Okay, so, just take note here. We have a list of everyone in the house or on the grounds at the time of Reverend MacDonald's death. We've decided that the reverend had no outside enemies. We don't believe Emil Roth is involved, but we'll keep looking. According to what we learned about Reverend MacDonald, it really seems likely that it was a tragic accident," Kelsey said.

"And that would be better than the alternative," Logan said.

Jane rose and walked over to a table where a bottle of champagne sat in a silver bowl of ice with crystal flutes around it. She didn't make a move to open the champagne. She spun around. "I say we go down for a cocktail hour and keep talking with whoever comes near us."

"Okay," Sloan said, rising again.

"Sure," Kelsey agreed.

"Who knows? Too bad there isn't a butler here," Logan said.

"There should have been a butler," Jane said.

"Because the butler often did it?" Kelsey asked.

Jane smiled. "No, it's a castle. There should be a butler. But—" Her voice trailed as she looked at Kelsey's board. "I wish that I believed that Reverend MacDonald just fell. But I don't."

"A hunch?" Kelsey asked her seriously.

They tended to pay attention to gut feelings. But, of course, everyone was wondering if Jane wasn't influenced by the circumstances here at the castle.

"We'll get images of everyone in the house and send them to the main office," Sloan said. "They can find out things about the past by just running searches, and it will be much easier for them to do that than us."

She smiled. "Yes, please. And maybe we can take a walk right before dinner and see if we can chat with any of the locals."

"The locals?" Kelsey murmured.

"Local ghosts," Jane said. "Who knows just what they might know?"

Chapter Five

"How is everyone doing?" Emil Roth asked as they entered the Great Hall.

He was there before them and held a crystal decanter of something dark in his hand. He waved it about as they entered. Jane thought he might have been there imbibing for some time.

"Brandy," he said, "anyone want to join me?"

"Club soda with lime?" Sloan asked him.

"Wise man," Roth noted. "Since people seem to trip down stairs around here. It's best to keep a clean and sober mind. I, however, will just crawl up the stairs. It's hard to trip when you crawl."

He set down the decanter and poured a soda for Sloan, but as he handed the glass over he was looking at Jane. He shuddered, then smiled. "I'm sorry. So sorry! Really. It's just you do bear a strange resemblance to Elizabeth Roth."

"Resemblances can be strange, of course," Jane said. "But sometimes it just depends on what angle an artist gave to a rendering."

"You know a lot about art?" he asked her.

"Jane is a wonderful artist," Kelsey said.

"I'm a forensic artist," Jane said.

He shuddered again. "You draw or paint dead people?"

"Sometimes. But, sometimes, I paint the living. When they're missing, if they have amnesia, if we need to get their images out to the public for a reason."

He gave a slightly sloppy smile. "So you could sketch me?"

"Certainly," she told him.

"Ah, yes. You could, but would you?" he asked.

"If you wish," she said.

"How rude of me. A tragic day. It should have been your wedding. And here I am, asking you to sketch me."

"I don't mind at all," Jane said.

"I'll run up and get your sketch pad," Sloan offered.

Emil lifted his glass to Sloan. "Don't run, not on those stairs."

"I'll be careful," Sloan promised.

"Do you need an easel? Is there something else I can get you? Draw what you really see, too, okay? I don't need to be flattered and I'd like a true image."

Logan pulled out a chair at the table for Jane as he told Emil, "Jane has a unique talent for catching expressions and what makes a person an individual. I'm sure what you'll get is honest."

Jane laughed softly. "I won't try to be unflattering."

Emil drew out the chair across from her. "Am I good here? Do you need more light?"

"I'm fine. As soon as Sloan brings down the pad, we'll be set to go," she promised.

"Please," Emil told Logan and Kelsey, "help yourselves to drinks. I believe Chef will send someone in with hors d'oeuvres soon."

"Thank you," Kelsey told him. "Jane?"

"Diet cola, thanks," Jane said.

"Ah, nothing more exciting?" Emil asked her.

"We're just not feeling all that festive, I guess," Jane said.

Sloan arrived with her sketch pad and a box of pencils. She smiled and thanked him.

"Ready when you are," Emil told her.

"I've already begun," she said.

"You're not drawing."

"But I am studying your face," she said softly.

"Ah," he said. "Should I pose? Lean in? Rest my chin on a fist?"

"No," she told him, picking up a pencil.

She began to sketch. To her amazement, she thought that it was one of her best, and quickly so. She changed pencils frequently, finding light and shadows. She caught his youth, something of a lost empathy in his eyes, and a world weariness he might not have expected. She also caught a bit of the handsome young Renaissance man. Or, perhaps, a rich kid adrift because he could probably be more than what the world seemed to expect of him. When she finished, she hesitated, looking at him.

"May I?" he asked.

"Certainly," she told him.

He took the drawing and studied it for a long time. "Could I possibly have this?"

"Of course," Jane told him.

"May I snap a phone pic of it?" Logan asked him. "It's really excellent. I'd love to have it, too."

"Yes, definitely," Kelsey said.

Mrs. Avery came walking into the room, her lips pursed. She seemed unhappy that Emil appeared to be enjoying his guests. Perhaps she was just unhappy that he was there at all.

"Will you have hors d'oeuvres soon?" she asked politely.

"Yes, we will, Denise. But, first, come here. You must see this!"

"Really, Emil—" Mrs. Avery began.

"Oh, come, come, Denny! Come over here and see this. You must sit, too, if Miss Everett is willing. I'm quite astounded by the likeness she created of me." Emil said.

"I have business—" Mrs. Avery began.

"Yes, yes, you do. You work for me. Sit for a spell. Jane, will you?" Emil asked.

"If you wish."

"Will this take long?" Mrs. Avery asked.

"Five minutes," Sloan said.

Jane thought there was something firm in his voice. He used a tone she knew, though it wasn't often directed at her anymore. People complied with that tone.

Mrs. Avery sat.

She began to sketch and caught the woman's high cheekbones and thin lips. Because it seemed that the sketch was coming out a little too harsh, she set a tiny stray curl upon the forehead and down the face. The sketch caught the true dignity of the woman, but softened her as well. Jane was surprised to see Denise Avery's face as she studied the drawing.

She looked up at Jane with a smile. "That's really nice. Thank you."

"And she'll let you keep it, Denny," Emil said. "After Logan snaps a pic, that is."

"I would love to keep it. Thank you," she said.

Before she could rise, Chef stuck his nose and then his body into the Great Hall. "May I begin with the service?"

"Oh, not until Miss Everett does a sketch," Mrs. Avery said. "Come, sit!"

Jane looked at Sloan.

He grinned at her with pleasure. Logan, she knew, would get a snapshot on his camera of every shot. That night, he'd get every drawing, along with names, to their base. Then they'd know if everyone was who and what they claimed to be.

Before they were done, she'd sketched everyone working at the castle except for the two maids who only came in from nine to five—Sonia Anderson and Lila Adkins. Before she finished with everyone, she asked Chef to bring in the hors d'oeuvres. And as he and his assistants, Harry Taubolt and Devon Richard, served the food, Sloan began speaking with them. By the time she was done with her last sketch for the night—that of Scully Adair—it was agreed that they would all—guests, owner, and employees—eat together that night in the Great Hall.

"It's nice to be together," Scully told Jane, sitting beside her.

The food was all on the table and they passed things around.

It had all gone surprisingly well.

"Considering the fact that a man died here just hours ago," Devon Richard said.

"An accident," Harry said. "It's awkward, isn't it? I mean, none of us really new the reverend, so we can't mourn him as if we lost a friend. And yet, he died here, and we're having dinner."

"People still have to eat," Mrs. Avery said.

"Yes, I know. And work and breathe and go on. It's just that I feel we should be mourning," Avery said.

"And things shouldn't go on as if they were so normal," Phoebe Martin said. Then she laughed uneasily. "Of course, this isn't normal. I've never dined in the Great Hall before."

"This is our way of mourning," Emil Roth said, and they were all quiet for a minute.

"We should say something," Chef announced. "I mean, it doesn't feel right. It just doesn't."

Sloan stood. He'd wound up across the table from Jane. "Shall we join hands."

They rose and did as he suggested. Sloan said a little prayer for Reverend MacDonald ending with, "May he rest in peace, a good man. He'll reside with the angels, certainly."

"Thank you," Emil said when he sat.

"The hall is quite something. But, I can see why you like to eat in your room, Mr. Roth, when you're here alone," Mr. Green said. Even he had been called in for a sketch and dinner.

"Of course, I do remember the days when the family was alive and cousins came from many different places, old aunts and uncles, too. Then, the place was alive with laughter, kids running here and there."

A silence followed his words.

"The castle is still a happy place," Mrs. Avery snapped. "You should hear the people when they come here. They love to laugh and to shiver! And our overnight guests are always delighted. Why, we have some of the best ratings to be found on the Internet."

"I wasn't implying that it wasn't happy," Mr. Green said. He looked quickly at Emil Roth. "I certainly meant no disrespect."

"None taken, my man," Roth said. "I say, pass the wine, will you, Phoebe? And do fill your glass first."

Phoebe looked at him, plucked up the wine, looked at him again, then poured herself a large glass.

Emil smiled at her and waited patiently.

Jane made a mental note that one of them would definitely make sure he got up the stairs okay that night. But as the wine flowed, the conversation became more casual. And when Chef and Harry headed to the kitchen to return with the dessert, Jane slipped away, determined to step outside for a few minutes. She headed out to the front. There were dangerous cliffs in the rear of the property, and she didn't intend to become a victim of the castle herself. She walked down toward the caretakers cottage where Mr. Green lived, then kept going, toward the guard house and Mrs. Avery's home.

She turned and looked back at the castle and saw the windows to her own room. They'd left the lights on. She stared upward for several seconds before her breath caught.

Someone in the room.

At one of the windows.

Watching her.

As she watched them.

* * * *

Jane was a special agent, the same as he was. She'd passed the academy and was in law enforcement. But she was still the woman he loved, the woman he was supposed to have married that day. So when Sloan realized Jane was out of the Great Hall, he followed. He didn't know why he felt such a sense of anxiety, but he did. He saw her, far down the path to the castle, as soon as he exited and came down the few stone steps at the entrance.

She was just standing on the path, looking back.

He hurried to her. She smiled as he came to her and pointed up at the castle.

"Someone is there," she said.

"Someone?" he asked.

"Were they all in the Great Hall?" she asked.

"When I left, yes."

"Then I believe Elizabeth does haunt our room," she said.

Sloan looked up. There was nothing there then.

She smiled. "No, I'm not losing it. Someone was there. Now, they're not."

"I believe you," he said.

"You know, I'm really not losing it in any way," she said, turning to him so that he slipped his arms around her. She smoothed back a lock of his hair. "I don't care where or when we marry one another. It doesn't matter. And it doesn't matter that we weren't married today. It does matter that a man died. A good man."

He smiled and nodded. "I know that."

Impulsively, he went down on a knee and took her hand. He kissed it both dramatically and tenderly and looked up to meet her eyes.

"I love you with the depth and breadth of my heart and soul. In my heart, you've already been my wife, my love, my soul mate, my life mate. Not to mention one hell of an agent. And artist, of course."

She laughed, drawing him to his feet and giving him a strong buff on the arm. "That started off so beautifully!"

"Hey, you are an amazing artist. And agent. You want to be an agent tonight, right?"

"I do," she told him. "It's just that speech, it could have stayed romantic."

"Want me to try again?"

"No!" She laughed. "I say we get back up there and make sure that Emil Roth makes it to his room."

"And then we'll make it to ours," he said.

"And then we'll make it to ours," she agreed.

Hand in hand, they made it back to the house. In the Great Hall, Mrs. Avery was saying that she needed to get some sleep. Chef told her that breakfast came early, and Phoebe Martin was headed upstairs, but when she saw Jane and Sloan come in, she stopped.

"Thank you so much, Jane, for the sketch. It's wonderful. And thank you both for somehow making a nice evening out of a horrible day. Good night. And don't forget, if you need anything—anything at all—we're happy to oblige."

"Thank you, Phoebe," Jane told her.

She scampered on toward the stairway. Jane followed her. As she did so, she heard Sloan and Logan talking to Emil Roth, convincing him that they'd see him to his room. It was time to sleep. The men and Kelsey were looking to see that Emil was safe. Jane followed Phoebe up the stairs, and then on up to the third floor.

Phoebe turned to look at her when she reached her door.

"Thank you," she said.

"You're welcome."

"You're worried about all of us."

"There was a lot of wine flowing down there at the dinner table."

But Phoebe looked at her with wide eyes.

"You don't believe that the reverend's death was an accident, do you?" she asked.

"Actually, we found out that he had a heart condition. That might have caused him to stumble. But we'll know more when the M.E. makes his report," Jane said.

But Phoebe still watched her. "That won't make any difference to you, will it? You think that he was killed."

Jane said, "The police seem to believe it was an accident."

"Do you think we're all in danger?"

"No," Jane said.

That wasn't a lie. Whoever the killer was, they were part of the castle crew. And the killer certainly wasn't in danger.

Phoebe shook her head. "Thank you for tonight."

"Of course," Jane said.

She left Phoebe to descend the stairs to the second level. Careful as she did so.

* * * *

Within another ten minutes, everyone was where they should be or on their way to their own homes. Sloan watched as Jane came down from the attic level, her hand firmly on the handrail of the far less elegant steps that led from the second floor to the attic. She joined him, Logan, and Kelsey on the second floor landing by their rooms.

"One of us will be up through the night. I'm taking first shift and Kelsey will be second. You two deserve to get some sleep or whatever tonight."

"We're fine," Sloan assured him.

"We know that," Kelsey said, grinning. "We just want you

to know that we're on the awake duty, or guard duty, or whatever you want to call it."

Sloan started to protest but Jane caught his arm. "Just tell them thank you, Sloan."

"Thank you," Sloan said.

Jane dragged him into the room.

"I'm, uh, up for whatever you're in the mood for," he said.

But she walked away from him, leaving him in the entry and heading into the bedroom. She stood there for a while and then walked back out.

"She's not here," she said.

"No?"

She shook her head with disappointment. "I thought that she would be. I thought that tonight we'd see her."

Sloan walked to her and took her gently into his arms. "Maybe she knows that we're here. Maybe she knows why we came. And maybe she's as good and sweet as history paints her. What she really wants is happiness for others."

She'd felt warm in his arms. Warm, soft and plaint, trusting, so much a part of him that their heartbeats seemed the same. But then she stiffened and pulled away from him. He realized that she was looking out one of the windows. The drapes hadn't been pulled closed. She walked to it and he followed closely behind her.

And he saw what she saw.

There was a man standing in the moonlight. He was by the caretaker's cottage, looking up. He seemed to be in breeches and a blousy poet's shirt. His hair was long, his thighs encased in boots.

"John McCawley," Jane whispered.

Sloan had to agree.

The figure in the moonlight faded.

Jane turned into Sloan's arms. "The past has something to do with this. I know it."

"We should get some sleep," he told her.

She nodded and headed into the bedroom. It was supposed to have been their wedding night. But he knew her. She was upset. The minister she'd brought to the castle had died here.

"I love you," she said.

"I know," he told her.

"I'll be in bed," she said. "Just give me a few minutes."

He let her go and walked over to the board Kelsey had set up that day, studying what she had written. *Who had something to gain from the death of a minister?*

He went over the names.

Mrs. Avery, he thought. The distant relative. The woman who had allowed Jane to book the castle for the wedding.

He walked into the bedroom. Jane hadn't even disrobed. She was lying on her side, her eyes closed, sound asleep. He laid down beside her and drew her into his arms. He held her as his mind whirled until he managed to sleep himself.

And then—

He woke.

He didn't know why. It was almost as if someone had shaken him awake.

But there was no one there.

Curious, he rose and walked back out to the foyer, then opened the door to the hall. Logan was opening the door to his room at the same time. Sloan looked down the other way. Someone was approaching Emil Roth's room in the darkness.

"Hey!" Sloan shouted.

The figure paused and turned to him. He could make out little of the person in the darkness. Whoever it was had bundled up in black pants, a black hoodie, and what even seemed to be a black cape of some kind. In the pale glow of the castle's night-lights, something gleamed.

A knife?

"Stop," Sloan demanded.

He stepped from his room, listening in the back of his mind for his door to close, for the lock to catch. He wasn't leaving Jane alone without a locked door. For a few seconds the figure stared at him and he stared back.

"Stop!" Sloan ordered again.

The figure began to run down the stairs at a breakneck speed.

Sloan raced after the person, Logan at his heels.

Chapter Six

Jane awoke to the sound of Sloan's voice, disturbed, aware she needed to be up. But she felt a soft touch on her cheek. Not the touch of a lover, rather the brush of gentle fingers that a mother, a sister, or a caring friend might give. For a moment she lay still, her Glock on the bedside table. If there was someone there, no matter how lightly they touched her—

She opened her eyes.

And saw Elizabeth Roth.

The ghost looked at her with sorrow and grave concern. And then, when she realized that Jane was awake, she vanished.

"No!" Jane said. "Please, help us. Don't go!"

But there were more shouts in the hallway and the apparition disappeared in a matter of seconds, fading from Jane's sight. Jane bolted up, grabbed her gun, and headed into the hall.

It was empty.

She cautiously moved out of the bridal suite. She backed her way to the door to Kelsey and Logan's suite and ducked her head in. Neither was there. Almost running, she made her way to Emil Roth's suite. The outer door was open. Taking every precaution, she pushed the door inward and made her way into the room. Like the bridal suite, it had an outer foyer area with a grouping of chairs and a wet bar. Roth family plaques adorned the walls along with prints of medieval paintings. She made her way through to the bedroom, pushed the door open, and quickly flicked on the light, hoping to first blind anyone who might have attacked Emil in the night, or who might be lingering in the room.

To her astonishment, Emil Roth was there.

And he wasn't alone.

She was awkwardly greeted by the sight of flesh. Way more of Emil Roth's pale body than she had ever wanted to see and a pair of massive, gleaming breasts. Way too much of a skinny derrière. Emil's flesh, a woman's flesh—sweaty, writhing flesh—writhing until she turned the light on and they both stopped moving like deer suddenly blinded by headlights.

The woman screamed.

Emil Roth roared. "What the hell?"

Jane instantly turned the light off. "Sorry—sorry! Your door to the hallway was open. I was afraid that someone was hurting you."

She heard the tinkle of the woman's laughter. And then, in the darkness, she realized she knew who the woman was.

Scully Adair.

"I wasn't hurting anyone, I swear!" Scully said. "But, please, don't say anything! Please, don't say anything to Mrs. Avery. I'll wind up fired—"

Scully started to rise.

Jane lifted a hand to her. "I won't say a word, I swear it. Please don't get up on my account. I won't tell Mrs. Avery a thing."

"Hey, now, I own the place," Emil said.

"Whatever!" Jane told them. "I will not say a word. It's between you all. Forgive me. Sorry, I'm out of here. Pretend I was never here. Just do what you were doing, I mean, um, you just might want to lock your door."

She flew back out of the room, shaking, slamming the door in her wake. The locks were automatic, she reminded herself. They'd been warned about that—step outside and it would catch behind you. For a moment, she leaned against the closed door. Visions stuck in her head that she prayed she could quickly clear.

She gave herself a mental shake.

If Emil Roth was fine, what was going on? Where the hell was Sloan? Where were Kelsey and Logan? She hurried to the stairway and gripped the banister tightly, looking behind and around her as she started down the stairs to the castle's foyer. Still, she saw no one. The giant double front doors to the castle were ajar. She walked outside. A moon rode high, the air was still, and a low fog lay gentle on the ground. There was a night-light coming from Mr. Green's cottage and a slightly lower light emitted from the guardhouse where Mrs. Avery was supposed to be sleeping. She wasn't sure why, but she walked the distance around the grounds, on alert, ever ready to be surprised by someone lurking in the night or watching and waiting. But no one accosted her. Instead, she felt as if she was being beckoned toward the chapel. She wasn't afraid of the dead. The dead had helped her many times. She made her way through the gate at the low stone wall that surrounded the chapel. She was afraid of the living. They were dangerous, in her mind.

But no one jumped up or slunk around from a gravestone or a tomb.

She reached the chapel door and pushed it inward. Someone was sitting in a pew, looking at the altar.

He rose.

She looked at John McCawley, tragically killed in a hunting accident the eve of his wedding.

He looked at her a long moment. "You see me? You see

me clearly?"

"I do," she told him.

He seemed incredulous, then he smiled, and she saw that he had been a truly handsome young man with a grace about him. "Forgive me. I see people pointing into the woods and saying that they see me when I'm standing next to them. And the ghost hunters! Lord save us all. A twig snaps and they scream, 'What was that, oh my God!'"

"There are several of us here who see the—" She paused. She wasn't sure why, but saying "dead" seemed very rude. "Who see those who have gone before us."

"Really? Amazing and wonderful. I heard one of the maids whispering about it today. You do look like my love, like my Elizabeth. Are you a descendant?"

"I'm really not. I'm sorry," she told him.

"Ah, well, no matter." He studied her anxiously. "If you see Elizabeth—I know she's here. I see her at the window. But you—you with this gift of yours, if you see her, tell her that I love her. I wait for her. I'll never leave her. I love her in death as I loved her in life."

"Why don't you tell her yourself?" Jane asked.

He shook his head. "It's as if I can't breach the castle. I try to enter. I don't know why. The family arranged the wedding, but they didn't want us together. There were a number of us out that day—Emil Roth, father and son, among them. I watched the blood flow from me, but I never knew who'd done the deed. And yet, I prayed that my love would go on— that Elizabeth would rally and find happiness. She loved me, but she wasn't weak. She should have lived a long life and she should have found happiness. But she did not. I'll never leave her now. I will watch her at the window for eternity."

"I'll tell her," Jane said. "But there is a way—there is always a way. We'll figure it out, and you two may tell each other everything you wish to say."

As she spoke, she heard her name cried out loudly and with anguish.

Sloan!

"Here!" she cried. "I'm in the chapel."

A moment later, the door burst in and Sloan rushed to her, sweeping her into his arms. He was oblivious to the ghost, oblivious to everything but her.

He shook as he held her.

"Hey," she said. "I'm fine. Where have you been? Where are Kelsey and Logan?"

"Right behind me. There was someone about to break into Emil Roth's room. We all chased whoever it was down the stairs and out into the yard, but they disappeared as if into thin air," Sloan said with disgust. "I went back to the room and then I banged on Roth's door and—Roth is sleeping with his help."

"I know," Jane said.

Logan came striding in, followed by Kelsey. "There you are," Kelsey said, pushing Sloan aside to give Jane a hug. "We were worried sick."

Jane told them, "Hey! You guys left me."

"We were chasing a mysterious figure," Logan explained.

"The door locked, right, when I left?" Sloan asked, worried.

She nodded. "I just came out looking for you." She frowned. "Hey—now, we're all out here and Emil Roth is back in his room."

They turned as if they were one and went racing back to the castle.

They weren't careful then as they raced up the stairs.

At the door to Emil Roth's suite, they suddenly paused. "Whatever he's doing, we have to interrupt him. We're trying to keep him alive," Sloan said.

Logan nodded and banged on the door. Emil Roth,

dressed in a silk robe, opened the door. Seeing them, he groaned. "You all again."

"Mr. Roth, someone was sneaking toward your door in the middle of the night. I believe they meant to cause you some harm," Sloan told them.

"It was me," said a squeaky, apologetic voice. Scully Adair, clad in an oversized shirt, her hair still in disarray, walked slowly out of the bedroom. She gave them a little wave. "Sorry. I'm so sorry."

Jane shook her head—trying to dispel unwanted images that rose before her mind's eye. "You don't need to apologize. You're both adults."

"But, Scully, it wasn't you," Sloan said. "It was someone wearing black, evidently sneaking around, who was headed toward Emil's door. We chased them, and whoever it was disappeared right outside the front door."

"Why would anyone want to hurt me? To most of the world, I'm worthless," Emil said dryly.

"You're not worthless!" Scully said passionately.

"You seem to be a fine enough young man, sincerely," Jane told him.

"But, beyond that, you are worth a fortune," Kelsey reminded him.

Emil Roth shook his head. "If I die, the only living heir— or heiress—is Denise Avery. But she doesn't just get everything. There are all kinds of trusts. The castle will be left to posterity. It will go to the village and be run by a trust and a group of directors."

"But she'd still make out all right," Logan said.

Emil waved a hand in the air. "She'd get a few million."

"Oh, Emil!" Jane said. "People have died for far less than a few million."

"But—Denise," Emil said.

Jane turned to Sloan. "Where was she when you all went

running after the figure into the night?"

"We woke up Mr. Green and Mrs. Avery," Logan said.

"But both took their time answering their doors," Sloan said.

"Which, of course, is more than possible when you're sound asleep," Kelsey said.

"This can't be—real," Emil said.

"We didn't imagine the figure we chased away," Sloan said flatly.

"So what do I do?" Emil asked.

"You sit tight," Logan said firmly. "We're waiting on some answers from our home office, and the M.E.'s report. We'll have that info in the morning. For tonight, sit tight. One of us will stay in the hall through the next few hours. When the sun comes up, you'll be with one of us through the day until we get to the bottom of this."

"Really?" Scully asked. "I mean, the police said that it was an accident when the reverend fell. And someone was running around the halls? It could have been the ghost."

"It wasn't a ghost," Sloan said flatly. "It was flesh and blood that tried to get to you tonight, Emil. Dressed in black, sneaking around. And a man died here less than twenty-four hours ago. Let's be smart about this."

Emil nodded. "Yes. Thank you."

"Let's do what we can with the rest of the night," Logan said. "I'll take the hall first." He glanced at his watch. "Each of us takes an hour and a half. That gives everyone a few hours of sleep before morning. Kelsey, you relieve me. Sloan and Jane, you'll be up last."

"I meant to go home," Scully murmured.

"You can't now," Kelsey said flatly.

"But I'll be in the same clothing and Mrs. Avery—"

"I do own the place," Emil said again.

"You're a little shorter than Kelsey, but about the same

size," Sloan said. "We'll get you some clothing. For tonight, sit tight."

They left Emil Roth and Scully Adair and adjourned to the hall.

"You know, we're forgetting people," Jane pointed out. "Chef lives over the old stables. I'm not sure where that is. And Phoebe Martin is up in the attic."

"The stables are down the hill and to the right of the gatehouse," Sloan said. "And the attic, you walked Phoebe up there tonight, right?"

"Doesn't mean she stayed there," Jane pointed out.

"But what would Phoebe or Chef have to gain from hurting Emil Roth?" Kelsey asked.

"The only one to benefit would be Denise Avery," Sloan said.

"But she was there, down at the gatehouse, when you banged on her door, right?" Jane asked.

"Oh, yes, spitting fire, warning us that she had the right to throw us out," Logan said.

"Let's get through the night," Sloan said. "And hope we get something to go on in the morning."

Logan turned to Kelsey. "Get some sleep. I'll wake you in a bit. And you two," he said to Jane and Sloan. "Go on in and—whatever. You have three hours."

Sloan slipped his hand to the base of Jane's spine and urged her toward their door. They entered and he waited for the click. He cupped her head between his hands and kissed her tenderly, the feel of his fingers feathering against the softness of her flesh an arousing touch. He had a talent for the right move at the right time. He could walk into a room and cast his head in one direction and she would just see that he was there and want him. He could be a joker. He could walk naked from a shower and tease and play and tell her that the offer was evident.

But, right now, he wasn't sure what was on her mind. He could always make her long for him.

"She's been here."

"What?" he asked her.

And she told him about waking up to the feel of something on her cheek, of Elizabeth being there and looking at her worriedly. She told him about John McCawley waiting in the church, forever watching the windows for his love.

"Why can't he come in the house?" Sloan asked her.

"Maybe he was never really invited inside—invited to be a part of the family," Jane suggested.

"Did you ask him about any of this?" Sloan asked.

"I didn't really have time. You screamed for me and he disappeared."

"We'll talk about this with the others tomorrow," he said. "And until then—" He paused, his fingers tracing a pattern down her cheek, his eyes focused on hers. "Until then, we'll get some sleep."

She smiled. "When this is over, let's go to an island. A resort. Maybe one of those all-inclusive ones. One where we have our own little hut on the beach."

"No ghosts," he said.

"No ghosts."

"Or Mrs. Avery."

"You think she's guilty?"

"She has the only motive," Sloan said. "Can you think of another?"

At the moment, she couldn't.

She kissed his lips with a promise for the future.

"Go to sleep," he told her. "I can't sleep anyway, right now. I'll take both our turns watching the hall. I'll be back in once it's full light. Logan will be up by then."

She headed into the bedroom, exhausted. She knew Sloan. He'd be pacing in the foyer area of their room for a while, thinking.

But she fell quickly asleep.

She awoke.

And felt Sloan's warmth beside her. She loved that she lay with him at night and woke with him in the morning. She even loved that they could disagree, even argue, that life with him was comfortable—and yet, she could see him, breathe his scent, watch him walk from the shower and want him as if they'd never made love before.

She rolled over to tell him that she loved him.

But never spoke the words.

A shrill scream pierced the castle's quiet.

Chapter Seven

"I guess that Mrs. Avery wasn't responsible," Sloan said.

The scene was a repetition of the previous morning. Only now, it was Denise Avery who lay at the foot of the stairs, her neck broken.

Sloan looked at Logan, who'd been on guard duty. "What happened?"

"She was never on the second level to descend to the first," Logan said, looking at them.

This time, it had been Scully Adair—dressed in one of Kelsey's tailored work suits—who'd made the discovery when she walked down the stairs. Her scream had alerted the castle. Now, everyone was there, including Mr. Green.

Chef and Harry and Devon rushed in from the hall to the kitchen. Phoebe Martin had come running from the Great Hall and the two day maids, Sonia Anderson and Lila Adkins, hurried from the office. It was chaos, everyone asking each other if they'd seen Mrs. Avery.

"Whoa!" Sloan shouted. "Stop. All of you!"

They went silent.

Phoebe stared at Sloan with fear. Scully Adair seemed to be in shock. Harry and Devon just looked sick.

Chef shook his head. "I knew I should have taken that job out at the really haunted hotel in Colorado."

Mr. Green just stood there, hat in hand, shaking his head.

"Sorrowful end. The reverend? He was a good man. Mrs. Avery? Not so much. Still, a sorrowful end."

"We're going to have to call the police," Jane said.

"Already dialing," Logan told them.

"Let's leave her as she lies for the M.E.," Sloan said. "We'll head into the Great Hall and wait for the police."

They obeyed like sheep. Chef, Harry, and Devon drifted to one side of the table—team kitchen. Phoebe Martin, Sonia, and Lila to the other side. Emil Roth—appearing to be in total shock—walked to his place at the end.

Scully looked at the room uncertainly. At last, she walked to the wall and sank down against it and seemed to curl into herself.

"Did anyone see her this morning?" Logan asked.

"I did," Mr. Green volunteered. "I saw her walking up to the castle from the guard house."

"Did you speak with her?"

"No," he said. Then, he added, "I only speak with her when I have to."

"We saw her—the three of us," Chef told them.

"Yeah," Harry said. "She came in telling us that if we were all going to get so chummy with the guests, Chef needed to plan cheaper meals."

"Nice," Scully muttered.

"Did you see her?" Jane asked the maids.

The three of them shook their heads.

"Not until she was there. At the foot of the stairs. But, I knew. The minute I heard Scully screaming, I knew," Phoebe said. She stared at Jane. "It's the ghost. She's angry. Elizabeth is angry. You tried to get married here when she couldn't. I think she's trying to kill you!"

Sloan cleared his throat. "I really don't think that Jane and the reverend and Mrs. Avery resemble one another in any way. Nor do I think that a ghost is killing people."

"So she just tripped?" Harry asked hopefully.

"Personally, I don't think so," Jane said matter-of-factly.

"But the reverend just fell yesterday!" Harry protested.

"And she fell today," Kelsey said.

"So, if she didn't just fall—" Harry began.

"Someone pushed her," Devon finished.

"And who would want to kill that old battle-ax?" Chef demanded sarcastically.

The police didn't knock, they burst right in. Detective Forester immediately looked at the FBI agents. "Four of you are still here—and another person is dead? What now?"

Everyone began to speak at once again.

Sloan assumed that Detective Forester was decent at his job. But he probably didn't deal with situations like this often. And Detective Flick, at his heels, merely followed the path that his boss took.

"Hey!" Sloan shouted. "Tone it down. Let the detective get his questions out in an orderly fashion."

They all went silent like errant school children.

"The ghost did it!" Phoebe said again. "The ghost did not want people getting married here. Maybe Elizabeth Roth didn't even want to hurt the reverend. He was just there and she had to stop the wedding. And so, to stop killing other people, she had to kill Mrs. Avery, who kept letting people try to get married here."

Forester stared at her as if she'd completely lost her mind.

"Who saw what happened?" Forester demanded.

"No one saw anything," Sloan said. "My co-workers and I were on the second floor. Scully Adair came down the stairs and found her."

"No one else was around?" Forester demanded of Scully.

Scully shook her head.

"Where were the rest of you?" Forester asked.

Mr. Green told him he'd never entered the house. Chef

and cook said that they'd been in the kitchen, but that she had been in to see them just moments earlier.

"We had just gotten here," Lila said.

"We rode in together," Sonia said.

"I was still up in my room," Phoebe said.

"So she just fell?" Forester said, bewildered. "Someone has to know something." He spun on Mr. Green. "Who can vouch for you?"

Green just looked shocked. "I'm always outside."

"And you?" he demanded of Phoebe.

She stared back at him in horror. "Miss Everett walked me to my room last night. Damn you! Why will no one listen to me? The ghost did it."

"I want this place shut down to the public immediately," Forester told Emil Roth. "And no one leaves."

He made the announcement as if that were the answer to the dilemma.

"I don't really have anywhere else to go," Mr. Green muttered.

They heard activity at the door. The medical examiner had arrived. Forester told the group to stay in the Great Hall. Sloan ignored the order, getting a nod from Logan, and followed out on the heels of the detective.

The medical examiner shook his head as he stared at the corpse. "I'll get her temperature for time of death—"

"We know the damned time of death," Forester snapped. "Can't you tell if she was pushed or not?"

"When I have time for an autopsy," the man snapped back.

"Doctor," Sloan asked. "Did you discover anything yesterday that might have caused the reverend to fall? I heard he had a bad heart."

The medical examiner looked at him and nodded. "He was a walking time bomb. There was damage to his heart. Whether that caused his fall or not, I don't know. But he didn't suffer a heart attack before he came crashing down the stairs. And Mrs. Avery, I think she was in decent health. She certainly appeared to be."

Sloan said, "But she didn't fall from the top of the stairs. We were out in the hallway on that landing and we didn't see her." He actually hadn't been on the landing himself. Logan had been there. But, to Sloan's knowledge, Logan never missed anything.

"She fell from midway up?" Forester asked.

"She had to have. She was never on the second floor landing," Sloan said.

"It's a broken neck for sure," the medical examiner said. "If you want to know more, I'll be able to tell you in a few hours. She'll be an immediate priority at the morgue."

Forester thanked him. The medical examiner looked at Sloan and nodded. He had the feeling that he'd be getting any information just as quickly as Forester.

"What do you have to say?" Forester asked, looking at Sloan.

"I don't know what is happening any more than you do," Sloan said. "But three people breaking their necks on a stairway in a matter of years—two of them within two days? I don't see that as accidents, nor as coincidences. Something is going on here."

"You are saying that these people have been murdered?" Forester asked.

"I'd say it's likely."

"And what do you say we do to find out what is happening?"

Sloan was surprised. Forester's anger was all bluster. He was bewildered. There were no knives involved, no guns, no gang wars, and no obvious motive for killing. A husband hadn't gotten too angry with a wife. A mistress hadn't suddenly turned on a man who'd promised to leave his wife and marry her.

And yet, people were dead.

"Detective, we've been researching everyone here. We expect some reports this morning. But, questioning the people here could prove helpful."

Forester nodded. "I'll do it. Whatever you find out, you'll tell me, right?"

"Of course. This is your jurisdiction. We just happen to be here. We're happy to help. But I need to get together with my team."

Forester nodded and seemed better equipped to take control. "I'll see the employees one by one in the Great Hall. You and your team may return to your rooms. I'll send the cooks and the maids to the kitchen and start with Mrs. Avery's assistant."

Forester walked ahead of Sloan to return to the Great Hall. When they were there, he announced his intentions. "Chef, you and your helpers stay together. Miss Martin, Miss Anderson, Miss Adkins, you will stay together, too. You're welcome to wait your turn in the kitchen. Mr. Roth, we'll have to speak with you, but you're welcome to return to your room until Detective Flick comes to bring you down. Please understand, no one is being accused of anything but we must ascertain what happened here. Therefore, I need to speak with all of you, one by one. Mr. Green, you may return to your apartment. Just be ready to speak to us when we call you."

For a moment, everyone was dead still. Then, Chef rose. "Coffee sounds damned good. And breakfast. Detectives? Should I plan for you, too?"

Sloan was surprised when Forester looked at him—as if for approval.

"Chef, it's kind of you to look out for everyone," Sloan said.

He motioned to Logan, Kelsey, and Jane. As the others shuffled out, except for Scully Adair, who looked like a caged mouse, he and the Krewe members made their way to the stairs and up to the bridal suite.

"It wasn't Mrs. Avery after all," Logan said dryly, stating the obvious.

"Whatever motive could there be?" Kelsey asked.

"Motives for murder," Jane mused. "Greed? That seems to be out. Revenge? Who would have a motive for revenge against the reverend and Mrs. Avery?"

"Jealousy," Logan put in.

"Love," Jane said.

They all looked at her.

"Unrequited love?" she said.

"But who loved whom and wasn't loved in return?" Kelsey asked.

"Let's see what they've gotten us from the home office," Logan suggested.

He sat at Sloan's laptop, found his mail, and ran through everything that had been returned. "I sent them copies of Jane's sketches from last night along with names and everything else, and so far no one has a criminal record. Mr. Green has been here all his life. Our host, Emil, had some trouble with drinking and being rowdy in college, but that doesn't suggest he'd become homicidal. The maids? Lila Adkins is taking college courses by night. She hasn't even had a parking ticket. Sonia Anderson is halfway through a community college now. She wants to be a nurse. Phoebe Martin took the job here years ago when she was divorced. She took it because she could live at the castle, according to the records. Chef? He had offers all over the place but Emil Roth really liked him—they met at a restaurant in Boston—and offered him a husky salary. The two cooks? Devon Richard has applied to the police academy—with good scores. He'll probably be hired on when they have a position. And Harry Taubolt plans on staying to study with Chef. He wants a food career." He looked up at the others again. "Are we certain that Lila and Sonia left the castle last night?"

"Their cars were gone," Sloan said.

"I think we can rule them out. But how do we narrow down the others?" Kelsey asked.

"We're looking at Emil Roth, Scully Adair, Chef, Harry Taubolt, Devon Richard, Phoebe Martin, and Mr. Green," Logan said.

"Except that we know Emil Roth and Scully Adair were in Emil's room when whoever we saw on the stairs was sneaking around the house last night," Sloan said.

"So Chef, Harry, Devon, Phoebe, or Mr. Green," Jane said.

"And Mr. Green was in the caretaker's cottage when we went there. But he had time to slip in. The main thing is that whoever had been in the house just disappeared, as if into thin air. We need to find out where he or she got in and out of the house," Sloan said.

"We could start a search—" Kelsey said.

"Or just ask," Sloan suggested.

"Emil Roth," Jane said.

* * * *

Jane wasn't sure why but she felt the need to be in the room alone. Not that Logan, Sloan, and Kelsey weren't as good as she was when it came to communicating with the dead, but, in her experience, the dead sometimes chose who they would and wouldn't communicate with.

This time, she was certain, it was her.

Kelsey went down to the kitchen to talk to the cooks and maids. Sloan and Logan went down the hall to speak with Emil

Roth about the architecture of the castle.

She sat quietly in the bedroom and said, "Elizabeth, I know that you're here. Please, speak with me. Tell me if you've seen anything, if you know anything that might help us."

The air didn't stir, and yet she felt that someone had heard her.

"I saw John McCawley last night," she said. "He wanted me to tell you that he loves you. That he'll never leave you. He watches you at the window. But you know that. That's why you go to the window. So that you can see him."

Slowly, Elizabeth appeared before her and walked to where Jane sat on the bed.

"I didn't kill myself," she said. "They said that I took the laudanum on purpose. My poor father believed that I did it myself. But, I did not."

That wasn't what Jane had expected to hear. "I'm so sorry. But who would have given you the overdose?"

"It was in the tea, I think," she said. "I believe it was my father's maid. She knew that father had no faith in John. Father was so mistaken. I hated his money. John hated his money. Everyone believes that if you have money, that's all that anyone wants. But I loved John. Maybe she believed that if John and I were both gone, and with mother gone, just my brother left… but she underestimated my father. He had loved my mother. There was no affair between them. And still, I'm certain that she tried her best. She had her brother kill John in the woods and make it look as if he'd been killed by my brother or my father! And then, of course, it was easy for her to make it look as if I were a suicide."

"What was the maid's name?" Jane asked her.

"Molly," Elizabeth said.

"What became of her?"

"My father fired her. She became uppity and thought she ruled the place. But he took care of her. He fired her and banned her from the property."

"And what did she do?" Jane asked.

"She left the house, cursing us all!"

"Did you know Molly's last name?" Jane asked.

Elizabeth shook her head.

Jane jumped up. "I have to get into your family's records."

"They're in the office. There's a display case there with the records from the 19th century."

"Thank you," Jane told her.

"How can that help?" Elizabeth asked her. "Our deaths were so long ago."

"I'm not sure, at the moment," Jane said.

She left Elizabeth and the room.

Greed was just one motive for murder.

But unrequited love and revenge were two others.

Chapter Eight

"There are no secret entrances to the castle," Emil Roth told them. "But, of course, don't forget, there are two back entrances."

"But they can only be reached by the back, right?" Sloan asked.

Emil nodded.

Sloan looked at Logan. Their disappearing figure of the night before could have circled around the castle and come in through one of the back entrances. But what then?

"And there are servants' stairs that go up to the second landing and the attic," Emil said.

"Of course," Sloan said, irritated that he'd forgotten that in old places like this there was bound to be a second set of stairs.

Okay, one mystery solved.

"What are you thinking?" Emil asked Sloan.

"I'm thinking that someone has really been planning on attacking you and is getting rid of others in the hopes of ruining your life."

Emil looked at Logan. "Do you agree with that?"

"That's where we need your help," he said.

"I swear to you, I'm not the best human being in the world, but I'm not the worst. I haven't hurt anyone in a vicious business deal. I support equal rights. I'm decent," he said. "Not to mention, the only people here are my employees and you people."

"Is there any reason, say, Mr. Green, would harbor you any resentment?" Sloan asked.

"Not that I know of. He's happy, I'm happy. He tells me what he should do, and I tell him to go ahead and do it."

"What about the maids?"

"I overpay them. They have it easy."

"And Scully?" Sloan asked. She'd been with him—in bed—but that could have been part of a ploy. Perhaps two people working together.

"Scully," he said. "I love her."

Sloan and Logan looked at one another.

"Does she have an ex-boyfriend?" Logan asked.

True, they were both grasping at straws.

"Not that I know about. We started seeing each other about three months ago. Honestly, that's why I slipped back here and didn't go to Africa. We needed more time together. We wanted to be sure, really sure that we wanted to be together forever. And we are sure."

"Why was she so worried about what Mrs. Avery would think?" Sloan asked.

"Because, if we weren't really certain she wanted to keep her job. You know, everyone would have thought that she was after my money. She was so afraid of that. She has a degree in hospitality, so she could work anywhere. She's been offered good jobs by the major chains. But she wanted to stay here. Her mom and dad are here. Her dad isn't well. But to think she wanted my money? That was just stupid!"

There was a tap on the door and Sloan opened it.

Detective Flick was standing there. "Detective Forester would like to speak with Mr. Roth now."

"Of course," Emil said.

He followed Flick out. Sloan and Logan came too, but Flick motioned for them to hold back.

"Detective Forester asked that you head to the morgue. The medical examiner called. He has something. We want you to go so we can keep the questioning here going."

Sloan looked at Logan, who lowered his head to hide a grin. More probable, the medical examiner had specifically asked that the two of them come.

"We'll head right there," Sloan said.

"If you'll be good enough to tell us where it is," Logan said.

Flick gave them directions, then hurried ahead to make sure Emil Roth made it down the stairs okay. Sloan strode quickly down the hall to tell Jane where they were going. But she wasn't in the bridal suite. He called her cell and she answered promptly.

"I'm in the office, looking at records."

"What are you thinking?"

"It's vague at the moment, but revenge is looking good."

"Who's taking revenge on whom?" he asked.

She laughed. "I don't know yet. But as soon as I do, I'll call you."

He hung up and he and Logan headed to the morgue. The village was quaint and small, but the morgue was state of the art. The reverend's body had already been claimed. Mrs. Avery remained. She looked small and thin lying on the morgue table.

"Here is what I want you to see," the medical examiner said.

They looked at the shaved head which revealed a dark bruising.

"I don't know about the reverend, but Mrs. Avery didn't take an accidental fall. She was struck on the head. And then she was pushed down the landing and the murderer was quite lucky. She broke her neck on the way down. Gentlemen, this is no accidental death. I'm classifying it a homicide!"

* * * *

Jane learned that Elizabeth's "Molly" was Margaret Clarendon. She'd been employed by Emil Roth from the time he'd moved into the castle until three months after the deaths of John McCawley and Elizabeth Roth. She'd died, unmarried, according to the records, sixth months after her dismissal, when she'd careened off a cliff. Whether she'd thrown herself off or fallen, there was no record. But her death had been labeled accidental. Had Margaret Clarendon thrown herself off the cliff? Remorseful for what she had done? Or bitter, because with all her machinations she'd failed to win the lord of the castle? No way to tell from the records. So Jane left the office and headed up the stairs again to the second level. As she climbed, she remembered to grip the handrail.

Halfway up, she ran into Scully Adair.

"Do you know anything?" Scully asked her anxiously.

"No, Scully, I'm so sorry. I wish I did."

"They questioned me forever. They think I'm a murderer!"

"Not necessarily, Scully. They have to question everyone like that," Jane assured her.

"They still have Emil in there," Scully said.

"He'll be fine," Jane said.

"I just wish he'd come out. They're talking to everyone so long."

"They're being thorough, listening for something someone might not even realize is a clue to what is going on."

"I'm going to get some coffee and something to eat. Do you want to come?" Scully asked her.

"I'll be there in a minute. I have something to check on," Jane said. "I promise, I'll be right along."

Scully nodded, then gripped the banister tightly as she went on down the stairs.

When Jane reached the bridal suite, she was alone.

Elizabeth was nowhere to be seen and Jane didn't sense her presence. She went straight to her computer and video-phoned Angela at the home offices of the Krewe in Virginia.

Angela was with the first Krewe of Hunters. She'd earned her stripes in New Orleans. She was now married to Jackson Crow, the field director for all Krewe agents. While Jackson managed most of their commitments, there was still their overall head, Adam Harrison, who'd first recognized those out there with special intuition—that ability to talk to the dead. He was an incredibly kind man with a talent for finding and recruiting the right people for his Krewe.

Angela came online. She was a beautiful blonde who looked like she should have starred in a noir movie.

"Anything?" she asked Jane.

"So much!"

Jane told her about the morning's events, then said, "I need you to do a search on a woman named Margaret Clarendon, who lived here in the mid-1800s. Find out anything you can about her—before and after she worked for the Roth family."

"What are you thinking?"

"Elizabeth Roth believes that she was murdered, and that her fiancé was murdered, too. She thinks she was killed by this maid."

"And that will help you now?" Angela asked.

"I think so," Jane said. "There's no one to benefit from Emil Roth's death or from him being ruined. There has to be another motive."

"And you think Margaret Clarendon, despite the fact that she might have been a murderess, felt that ill was done to her?"

"We've seen it before. Sometimes there's a descendant out there who feels that they have to right a family wrong," Jane said.

"But remember that sometimes people just act on greed,

jealousy, or revenge. Modern day psychos or self-centered asses," Angela reminded her.

"I'll watch from all sides," Jane promised her.

She said good-bye and they cut the connection. Jane drummed her fingers on the table for a minute, and then hopped up again. She was going to have to wait for results, but she couldn't sit idly by.

Time to try to pay a visit to John McCawley again.

* * * *

"Here's what I can't figure. If Mrs. Avery was hit on the head, she had to have been hit on the head with something. Where is that something she was hit with?" Sloan asked.

"Whoever hit her took it with them," Logan said.

Sloan was the one driving as they headed back to the castle. He saw a coffee shop and switched on his blinker, ready to pull into the lot.

"We're stopping for coffee," Logan said.

Sloan grinned. "I thought we'd try for a little more gossip."

"Sounds good to me. And coffee, too," Logan told him.

They went in and were noticed right away by the hostess, who stood at the cash register. A number of patrons were sitting around at the various faux-leather booths. They were definitely the outsiders, probably known as the people who were the guests at the castle. Where bad things happened.

"Sit anywhere?" Sloan said, smiling at the cashier.

"Wherever," she said.

He and Logan claimed a booth. A waitress came over, offered them menus, and took their orders for coffee. She scampered away, then returned quickly. She looked as if she was both anxious and afraid to talk to them.

She flushed as she poured the coffee and caught Sloan's eyes. "I'm sorry. I mean, it's a small village. You're guests at the castle, right?"

"Yes, we are. Sad business there, though," Sloan said.

"My God, yes! The poor reverend. Everyone loved him, you know. And now they say that Mrs. Avery has fallen down the stairs and broken her neck, too!"

Her nametag identified her as Genie.

"Yes, Mrs. Avery died," Sloan said.

"The poor woman," Logan agreed.

The cashier, apparently, couldn't stand being out of the know. She headed over to the table with a bowl of coffee creamers.

"Poor woman, my foot," she said. "Denise Avery thought she was better than anyone in town. She really thought Emil would run himself into the ground with drugs, or his stupid bungee jumping, or parachuting or whatever. He fooled her."

Sloan and Logan glanced at one another and up at the cashier. Her tag noted her name as Mary.

"Oh, I know!" she said. "I must sound horrible. But she came in here all the time and was rude."

"I applied to work at the castle," Genie said. "She looked at me as if I were flypaper. I didn't stand a chance. I wasn't pretty enough."

"You're quite pretty!" Sloan told her.

Which was true.

"Oh, no! Mrs. Avery wanted really pretty girls to work there. Even as maids. I mean, who cares what your maid looks like if she does a good job?"

"Hmmph!" Mary said. "That woman wanted to tease Emil. She wanted to get him going with whoever she brought in. And then remind him, of course, that he had a position in life, even if he wasn't fulfilling it. She just wanted to mess with that man."

"She's gone now," Genie reminded her.

Mary crossed herself. "It's not good to speak ill of the

dead."

"But truth is truth," Genie said. "The reverend? He was a good man."

"Bad heart, though," Mary said.

"Oh, dear!" Genie said. "We are terrible. What would you like to eat?"

"What's fast?" Sloan asked.

"The special. Stew," Genie said.

"We'll take it," Logan told her.

"Sounds delicious," Sloan said.

It was actually terrible, or maybe it just seemed terrible because they'd been eating Chef's food. But it was fast and filling and they were out of there in no time. Sloan wasn't sure what they'd gained, but they'd gained something.

"Mrs. Avery was quite a manipulator," Sloan said.

"She was so determined to seduce Emil Roth with the maids, but he went and fell in love with Scully Adair," Logan mused.

Sloan looked at him. "Do we know what happened before he fell in love with Scully Adair?"

"It would be interesting to find out," Logan said.

* * * *

Jane was amazed at how quickly the day ended and darkness fell. It seemed that they'd just awoken with Mrs. Avery at the foot of the stairs. Then the police had come and begun their investigation. She had spoken with Angela, Kelsey had hob-knobbed with the kitchen staff and maids, and Logan and Sloan had headed to the autopsy. The hours had flown by, and as she came down the stairs, she could hear Detective Forester in the Great Hall. He'd certainly taken a long time with every single person who'd been in the house. She listened a second and realized from the slow answers he was receiving that Forester was now questioning Mr. Green. She thought about stopping by the kitchen, but decided to head on to the chapel.

She needed to talk with John McCawley.

She headed out again, just as she had the night before. There was no moonlight yet, the autumn sun fading, a brooding darkness hanging over the cliffs brought on by an overcast sky. She'd exited by the front to avoid running into anyone at the rear. She walked around the castle, from the manicured front to the wild and atmospheric rear, and hurried to the chapel.

John McCawley was waiting in front of the altar, staring up at it.

"Did you see her?" he asked, turning. "Did you see my Elizabeth?"

"I did," she told him. "And I told her and, of course, you know that she loves you. She thinks she was murdered. She didn't kill herself."

"What?" he asked.

"She believes that there was a maid at the house— Margaret or Molly—who wanted her father's attention. And that Molly believed that she could start by ridding the world of the two of you. And Molly had a brother—"

"David," John told her. "He was always coming to the stables, asking for any extra work."

"She believes that David shot you and that Molly poisoned her."

"Can you prove it?"

"Probably not after all these years," Jane said. "But you know. The two of you know. Maybe that's enough."

His face darkened and he began to frown. Jane thought that she had said something that disturbed him. But then she realized that he was looking behind her.

She spun around.

And saw a figure dressed in black.

She started to draw her Glock, but before she could something came hurtling at her. Ghosts didn't have much strength—thus the tales of rattling chains and squeaking floors and chairs that rocked themselves. But they did have something. And Jane was sure that John McCawley had used all of his strength to cast himself before her. She dove behind one of the pews, drew her gun, and fired. The solid *thunk* she heard confirmed that her bullet had found the wood of a pew.

She rolled and took aim again.

But there was no one there.

The wraith in black was gone, and so was John McCawley.

She rose. Her phone was ringing.

Angela.

She answered, watching the door to the chapel.

"I found out more about your Margaret Clarendon," Angela told her. "She does have a descendant working at the castle now."

Chapter Nine

Detective Flick was waiting for Sloan and Logan when they entered the castle. He immediately directed them to Detective Forester, who had set up in the Great Hall. They sat and told him what they'd discovered at the M.E.'s office.

"We're going to need a search warrant," Forester said. "We need to find whatever object carries Denise Avery's blood."

"You don't need a warrant."

Emil Roth stood at the arched entry to the Great Hall.

"I own the property. I give you my permission to search every room. I believe there's a legality about guests in rooms, but I believe my guests will give you permission, too. Am I correct, gentlemen?"

"Of course," Logan said.

"Then I'll call in some backup," Forester said, "and we'll get to it tonight."

"I think that's an excellent idea," Logan said.

"Where are Kelsey and Jane?" Sloan asked.

"Kitchen, I believe," Forester told them.

Logan and Sloan headed out of the Great Hall to the kitchen. Kelsey was sitting there with Chef and Harry and Devon.

"Something to eat?" Chef asked.

"No, thanks. We had some horrible food in town," Logan

told him.

Chef grinned. "I do have the reputation for being the best around."

"I'd not argue it," Logan assured him.

"Why would you stop in town when you're staying here?" Chef asked. "And how were you out when the rest of us are prisoners here? Oh, yeah, I forgot. You're Feds."

Logan slid into a seat at the kitchen table. "We went to hear gossip."

Sloan remained standing. He still didn't know where Jane was. "We heard a lot of interesting gossip. Apparently, not many people liked Mrs. Avery. In fact, they seemed to think that she was trying to make everything in the world go wrong for Emil Roth."

Chef shrugged. "She treated him like he was a kid. When he hired me, not long after his dad died, they had a huge fight. I overheard them. She told him that he didn't have the know-how to run anything and that he shouldn't make decisions without her. I'm surprised he didn't kill her. He was the heir, but she acted like she owned everything."

"But he didn't kill her, did he?" Sloan asked.

"Emil?" Harry asked. "He's a decent guy. He's like a regular guy, but with money. He'd be normal as hell if people like Mrs. Avery didn't keep telling him that he had responsibilities as if he were Spiderman or something."

"Where's Jane?" Sloan asked them.

Kelsey, who'd been sitting at the table, frowned. "I'll go see."

"Wait. I'll just try her phone," Sloan said.

He dialed Jane's number and listened as they continued to talk.

"The people in town even seemed to think that Avery hired only attractive maids to try and get Emil involved with them," Logan said.

"Was that her plan?" Harry asked.

"I never had it figured as an actual plan," Devon said. "Go figure. That dried up old prune of a biddy setting Emil up for sex!"

"Did it work?" Logan asked

"At first, maybe. A few girls wound up being fired for various infractions. Oh, never for flirting with or co-habiting or whatever you want to call it," Chef said. "They'd be fired for failing in their duty, for disturbing a guest, things like that."

Logan heard an unspoken *but.* "What?"

"That all ended a few months ago," Devon said.

"Just spit it out, they know everything," Harry said. "They're Feds, remember? Emil is crazy about Scully Adair. And Scully is crazy about him. I don't know how they were managing to hide it from Mrs. Avery. All the rest of us knew."

"But, he did see people before that?"

"Yeah, sure. He's young, good-looking, rich. Who wouldn't have seen him?" Harry asked.

Jane's phone was ringing and ringing with no answer. Sloan ended the call and looked at Logan and Kelsey.

"Now we go and find Jane," he said. "She's not answering, and I'm pretty sure I know who we're looking for. Kelsey, go get the detectives. Logan, will you search the house? I'm heading out to the chapel."

"What can we do?" Chef asked.

"Stay put," Sloan told him.

* * * *

Jane cautiously stepped out of the church. The overcast sky seemed to have fallen closer to the ground, a dense fog rising to meet it. The graveyard, benign by day, now seemed to hold dozens of places to hide. Winged angels cast shadows over crooked stones. Trees grew at a slant and gargoyles loomed over tombs, warding off all evil. Standing in the doorway for the chapel, she was in clear view.

"You know I have a gun and I do know how to use it," she said, addressing the graveyard. "You might as well come out. I'm sure that you want me to think that Scully Adair is doing all this. After all, you know that Scully is a descendant of Margaret Clarendon. And you must have heard that there were a few references to the fact that Margaret was suspected of having helped Elizabeth along to her death. But, you know what? I don't think that Scully herself knows that she has any relationship to the castle. Margaret's child with Emil Roth went up for adoption. We only found out the truth because we have access to all kinds of records. Phoebe, you were good. I mean that scream you let out when you *found* Reverend MacDonald was really something. And the shock in your eyes? Amazing. So, you had an affair with Emil Roth. You thought you were the one. And I don't believe that you did kill Cally Thorpe. That was really just a tragic accident. But if people started dying at every wedding, that would give the castle a real reputation. But that wasn't enough. You figured you'd get rid of Mrs. Avery. Make it really ghostly. You hated her, because she sucked you in. She fed you the story about Scully and her being a descendant of Margaret. You thought you'd replay history, except this time you'd win!"

Jane barely ducked in time as a piece of broken plaster wing off a cherub came flying her way. By the time she was up again, her quarry had moved. Slinking low, she ran from one tomb to the next.

"Phoebe, my Krewe will have figured it out by now, too. Killing me will get you nowhere. Nor is there anywhere for you to go. You'll be arrested, and you'll face murder charges. If you give yourself up right now, I can try to help you."

Jane had moved away from the chapel a fair distance. Phoebe was leading her to the rear, a place where the graves began to ride down the slopes off the cliffs. She raised her head, trying to see in the near darkness. She thought she heard something—coming from behind her.

She was certain that Phoebe was before her!

Something thumped into the gravestone she'd ducked beneath.

An arrow.

She heard laughter from the fog-riddled graveyard before her, eerie in the strange dying light and the cool air.

"No one gets married here! They don't marry here. They *die* here!" Phoebe called to her.

Jane thought she heard a snapping sound on the ground, coming closer. She rolled quickly and slunk on the ground, staying low. She was armed and she could aim. But she couldn't make out a damned thing to shoot at.

"Brides die!" Phoebe cried, laughing.

The sound was both ahead and behind Jane.

In fact, it seemed to come from all around.

* * * *

Sloan was quickly on his feet, racing to the back of the house. At the rear exit from the kitchen, he thought that he felt someone behind him.

He turned.

And she was there. Elizabeth Roth.

She stared at him with a drawn face and worried eyes.

"I'll find her!" he promised.

"The fog has fallen," Elizabeth said.

"I'll find her!" he said. "Come with me?"

"I can't leave the house."

"Try."

She shook her head.

He couldn't wait.

He bolted out of the castle and was instantly astounded by the pea soup of New England fog he found himself within. He could still see the spire of the chapel, so he headed toward it. He made his way through the gate, down the path, and threw the chapel door open.

Jane wasn't there.

But he heard something.

Laughter.

Eerie in the strange fog. It seemed to come from the left, and then from the right.

"Jane!" he shouted. "Jane!"

He heard her reply.

And as he did, he realized that shouting had been a mistake. She was might be risking her life to shout out a warning to him.

"It's Phoebe and someone else, Sloan! Someone else with a bow and arrow, hunting us down," Jane shouted back to him.

He dropped to the ground just as something whizzed by his head. He tried to calculate the source of the arrow that had come his way. But whoever was shooting with a bow and arrow was now halfway around the church.

The laughter had come from the far rear.

On his hands and knees, he crawled around the graveyard.

* * * *

Jane tried to determine where she was, but with the distance they'd come she thought she might be in the back of the chapel, near the cliffs.

"I'm going to get you!" Phoebe said, her voice startlingly near.

She couldn't see anything. So how could Phoebe?

She didn't reply.

Then Phoebe began to chant. *"Good girls die, the bitches lie, the brides go straight to decay. This time round, the good girl dies and the bitch's lies will let her win the day!"*

"How do you see this as winning?" Jane cried out. "Emil is seriously in love with Scully. He'll marry her and you'll go to jail."

"Not true. Scully is right here with me. And if you don't show yourself now, she's going over the cliff!" Phoebe cried.

"I don't believe you. Scully was in the castle."

"She's here now. Wanna hear her scream?"

Jane heard a muffled cry.

Scully.

She winced, bracing against a gravestone.

"If you don't come out, she goes over the cliff right now!"

Sloan was out there, too, she thought. He had to be.

She'd be all right.

Or would she?

* * * *

Sloan kept silent and crept along the earth.

Another arrow flew past. That one, he was sure, had been sent blindly. He crept for what seemed like a lifetime but, looking at his watch, he saw that two minutes had passed. Another arrow flew by. This time he saw the arch and pattern.

He crept in the right direction.

Slow and silent.

At last he found himself behind the archer.

He waited and watched, forcing himself to be patient.

When the archer went to string another arrow, he pounced.

And together, they started rolling downhill.

* * * *

Jane realized there was nothing to do but stand. Her Glock was tucked into the back of her jeans.

"I'm here," she cried.

"Come out where I can see you!" Phoebe demanded.

"Where is that?"

"Come closer to my voice."

She did as told and tripped once over a broken stone, but then she saw images appear before her. Phoebe had somehow taken Scully hostage. She stood with Scully, close to the edge of the cliff, and held a knife to her throat.

"Drop the gun," Phoebe said.

"Let Scully go first," she said.

"Drop the gun, or she goes over."

"You're going to die or go to prison," Jane said.

Phoebe shook her head. "You'll be dead. And the whole thing will look like the crazy Krewe of Hunters unit—the *ghost unit*—went off the deep end and killed everybody. Then Emil will come back to me. He's young and sweet and pliable. He'll love me again."

"You were never anything but an affair to him, Phoebe. He loved Scully from the start."

"Put the gun down. She's already bleeding," Phoebe warned.

Should she pretend to do as instructed, then shoot? She could aim for Phoebe's head, but if either woman moved—

Someone lightly touched her.

And she heard a whisper that seemed part of the fog.

"Your love is behind you. Duck down. I'll do what I can."

Jane reached for her gun, dropped to the ground, and told Phoebe, "She's coming for you."

"Who?"

"The ghost of Elizabeth Roth. She's disgusted with what you're doing, trying to use the past to make a mockery of the present. She's there. At your side. Can't you feel her? She's touching you now."

"You're full of—" Phoebe began and broke off.

Elizabeth Roth was there, standing next to Phoebe, touching her hair.

Jane flew to her feet, sprinted forward, and caught Phoebe and Scully together, bringing them all down.

They landed hard, but Scully was free.

"Get up and run!" Jane ordered.

Thankfully, Scully had the sense to obey.

Phoebe still held her knife. She jumped to her feet in a fury, knife raised, ready to leap to where Jane had fallen.

But a shot rang out.

Phoebe paused midair. Then her body was propelled backward, disappearing into the fog. Jane heard her scream until a distant thud, flesh impacting rock, silenced everything.

An unearthly quiet returned.

Then shouts everywhere.

Logan and Kelsey. Forester and Flick. Chef and Harry and Devon and Lila and Sonia. All coming from the castle. Someone walked out of the fog toward her, gun in hand. Impossibly tall and broad and wonderful and always there for her. Her partner, in life, in work, and in breathing. Sloan didn't speak as he drew her to her feet and into his arms.

He just held her.

And their hearts beat together.

* * * *

"But, Mr. Green?"

It was Emil who seemed the most shocked. He'd trusted the man, thought he'd had a champion in him.

It was nearly morning again.

And, as the survivors gathered in the Great Hall while Forester's crew worked to find the bodies down the cliff, Sloan knew they were all grateful to know that there wouldn't be another one at the foot of the stairs that morning.

"Why Mr. Green?" Emil repeated.

"I think he just became involved with Phoebe. When you stopped seeing her, she started planning her revenge. I think she was trying to find a way to make her past part of yours. Instead, she discovered that Scully is a distant relative," Jane said.

"And," Sloan explained, "once she'd come up with her plan, she knew she needed help. And poor Mr. Green, alone and lonely. He was no match for Phoebe. He did what she told him. I believe she had him convinced that she had to do what was right for you and if so, she'd be with him forever and ever."

"But she wanted me," Emil said, confused.

"She didn't tell Green that part. She took care of the killing herself. But she needed him to help when it came to getting rid of you and Scully."

"As if she'd have ever gotten away with it," Logan muttered angrily. "The Krewe of Hunters doesn't lose. We come on harder and harder until a case is solved."

"We'll never really know what was on Green's mind, will we?" Kelsey asked.

Sloan lowered his head and shook it.

When he'd tackled Green, he'd subdued him and tied his hands. He'd never suspected, though, that the bound man would pitch himself over the cliff. But that's exactly what had happened once Green realized Phoebe was gone. He looked up. Logan was watching him, knowing what he was feeling.

"We try to save the victims first and always," he said.

"You saved Scully for me," Emil said.

Sloan decided not to tell him that Jane had saved Scully. He'd saved his own love and his own life with a well-placed shot.

"What will happen now?" Jane asked. "With this place?"

"I think I'll close it," Emil said. "Funny, I always dreamed I'd be married here one day. I'm not huge on tradition, but my parents were married here."

"I think you should be married here," Jane told him. "Prove to the world that the castle isn't evil. Only people can be evil. Make the castle a place of joy."

"She's right," Scully said.

"We get to be bridesmaids!" Lila said.

"Oh, yes! Except, of course, we get to be in on picking the dresses," Sonia added.

"You'll need a best man," Chef told Emil.

"And ushers," Harry said.

Detective Forester stood. "I'll at least expect an invitation. And one for Flick, too, of course."

"You got it," Emil promised. He looked at Jane. "But, you did plan to have your wedding here, you know?"

"But we're not the lord and lady of the castle," Jane said.

"I think we'll be headed for an island in the Caribbean," Sloan told him.

"You'll always be welcome here," Emil told them. "And anywhere I have holdings. And, I know that with Scully at my side, I'll make good. And we'll do good things. I swear it!"

"I believe you will," Sloan assured him.

"Flick and I will be leaving now," Forester said.

"I'll walk you out," Sloan offered.

Jane stood as he did. He smiled at her. They were both still muddy and grass-stained. They might not be married at the castle, but he did intend to make good use of the elaborate shower in the bridal suite as soon as he could.

They walked to the door and out onto the front lawn.

Emil was going to need a new caretaker, too.

But, as they waved good-bye to the detectives, Sloan was certain he'd never seen the place more beautiful.

Elizabeth Roth had realized that she could leave the castle. She stood with her beloved John down at the gates, oblivious to all else. She and John didn't notice the car that drove by them. They were engaged in a long kiss. And as the car passed, the sun rose high above them, crimson rays of extraordinary light raining down, more like twilight than dawn.

Sloan lifted a hand to shield his eyes, blinking against the glare.

When the light shifted, they were gone.

"Do you think—?" Jane asked.

"I don't know. But I do know they're together."

"Like we'll always be," she said.

"Shower," he said. "And then—"

"We'll fool around?"

"Isn't that how all of this started?"

That it was, she thought.

"Then, off to the Caribbean," he said. "Some place warm, with lots of blue water and sunshine. And we'll fool around for a lifetime."

She lifted her dirt-smudged face to his.

And he kissed the most beautiful lips he'd ever seen.

Sign up for the 1001 Dark Nights Newsletter
and be entered to win a Tiffany Key necklace.
There's a new contest every month!

Visit www.1001DarkNights.com/key/ to subscribe.

As a bonus, all subscribers will receive a free
1001 Dark Nights story on 1/1/15.
The First Night
by Shayla Black, Lexi Blake & M.J. Rose

Turn the page for a full list of the
1001 Dark Nights fabulous novellas...

1001 Dark Nights

FOREVER WICKED
A Wicked Lovers Novella
by Shayla Black

CRIMSON TWILIGHT
A Krewe of Hunters Novella
by Heather Graham

CAPTURED IN SURRENDER
A MacKenzie Family Novella
by Liliana Hart

SILENT BITE: A SCANGUARDS WEDDING
A Scanguards Vampire Novella
by Tina Folsom

DUNGEON GAMES
A Masters and Mercenaries Novella
by Lexi Blake

AZAGOTH
A Demonica Novella
by Larissa Ione

NEED YOU NOW
by Lisa Renee Jones

SHOW ME, BABY
A Masters of the Shadowlands Novella
by Cherise Sinclair

ROPED IN
A Blacktop Cowboys ® Novella
by Lorelei James

TEMPTED BY MIDNIGHT
A Midnight Breed Novella
by Lara Adrian

THE FLAME
by Christopher Rice

CARESS OF DARKNESS
A Phoenix Brotherhood Novella
by Julie Kenner

About Heather Graham

Heather Graham has been writing for many years and actually has published nearly 200 titles. So, for this page, we'll concentrate on the Krewe of Hunters.

They include:

Phantom Evil
Heart of Evil
Sacred Evil
The Evil Inside
The Unseen
The Unholy
The Unspoken
The Uninvited
The Night is Watching
The Night is Alive
The Night is Forever

(All available through Amazon and other fine retailers, in print and digital—and through Brilliance Audio as well.)

Actually, though, Adam Harrison—responsible for putting the Krewe together, first appeared in a book called *Haunted*. He also appeared in *Nightwalker* and has walk-ons in a few other books. For more ghostly novels, readers might enjoy the Flynn Brothers Trilogy—*Deadly Night*, *Deadly Harvest*, and *Deadly Gift*, or the Key West Trilogy—*Ghost Moon*, *Ghost Shadow*, and *Ghost Night*.

Out next for Heather the second book in the Cafferty and Quinn series, *Waking the Dead*—which follows *Let the Dead Sleep*. Go figure! (I guess they've slept long enough!)

The Vampire Series (now under Heather Graham/ previously Shannon Drake) *Beneath a Blood Red Moon, When Darkness Falls, Deep Midnight, Realm of Shadows, The Awakening, Dead by Dusk, Blood Red, Kiss of Darkness,* and *From Dust to Dust.*

For more info, please visit her web page, theoriginalheathergraham.com or stop by on Facebook.

The Night is Watching
Krewe of Hunters
By Heather Graham
Now Available!

Chapter 1

Jane Everett was entranced.

She'd been to a ghost town or two in her day, but never a functioning ghost town.

But then, of course, Lily, Arizona, had never really been a ghost town because it had never been completely deserted. It had just fallen by the wayside. It had seen good times—when the mines yielded silver and there'd been a hint of gold, as well, and the saloons and merchants had flourished—and it had seen bad times when the mines ran dry. Still, it had the look of either a ghost town or the set of a Western movie. The main street had raised wooden sidewalks and an unpaved dirt street. Muddy when it rained, she was certain, but that was seldom in this area.

The car her boss, Special Agent Logan Raintree, had hired to bring her to town let her out in front of the Gilded Lily, where she'd be staying. The driver had set her bag on the wooden sidewalk, but she waited a minute before going in, enjoying a long view of the street.

There were a number of tourists around. She heard laughter from across the street and saw that a group of children had come from a shop called Desert Diamonds and were happily licking away at ice cream cones. Farther down, a guide was leading several riders out of the stables; she could hear his voice as he began to tell them the history of the town.

But the theater itself was where she was heading so she turned and studied it for a moment. Someone had taken pains to preserve rather than renovate, and the place appeared grand—if *grand* was the right word. Well, maybe grand in a rustic way. The carved wooden fence that wound around the roof was painted with an array of lilies and the name of the theater; hanging over the fence and held in place with old chain were signs advertising the current production, *The Perils of Poor Little Paulina*. Actors' names were listed in smaller print beneath the title. She knew the show was a parody of the serialized *Perils of Pauline* that had been popular in the early part of the twentieth century.

No neon here, she thought, smiling. They were far from Broadway.

She'd read that the Gilded Lily had hosted many fine performers over the years. The theater had been established at a time when someone had longed to bring a little eastern "class" to the rugged West; naturally, the results had been somewhat mixed.

As she stood on the street looking up at the edifice, a man came flying out the latticed doors. Tall and square as a wrestler, clean shaven and bald with dark eyes and white winged brows, he bustled with energy. "Jane? Jane Everett? From the FBI?"

"Yes, I am. Hello."

"Welcome to Lily, Arizona," he said enthusiastically. "I'm Henri Coque, artistic director of the theater for about a year now and, I might add, director of the current production, *The Perils of Poor Little Paulina*. We're delighted to have you here."

"I'm delighted to be here," she responded. "It's a beautiful place. Who wouldn't want to come to a charming, Western, almost ghost town?"

He laughed at that. "I'm glad to hear that, especially since I'm the mayor here, as well as the artistic director. Lily itself is small. Let me get your bag, and I'll show you around the theater and take you to your room. I hope you're all right with staying here. Someone suggested one of the chain hotels up the highway, but everyone else thought you'd enjoy the Gilded Lily more."

"I'm happy to be here," Jane assured him. "I can stay at a chain hotel anywhere."

She *was* happy. They'd been between cases when Logan had heard from an old friend of his—a Texas cop, now an Arizona sheriff—that a skull had appeared mysteriously in the storage cellar of a historic theater. It had sounded fascinating to her and she'd agreed to come out here. The local coroner's office had deemed the skull to be over a hundred years old and had determined that handing it over to the FBI was justified, so that perhaps the deceased could be identified and given a proper burial. Like most law enforcement agencies, the police here were busy with current cases that demanded answers for the living.

The skull, she knew, was no longer at the theater. She would work at the new sheriff's office on the highway, but she was intrigued by the opportunity to spend time at the historic theater, learn the history of it and, of course, see where the skull was found.

That was the confusion—and the mystery. No one remembered seeing the skull wearing the wig before. Granted, the theater had been holding shows forever; it had never closed down. And people had been using the various wigs down there forever, too. From her briefing notes, Jane knew that everyone working at the theater and involved with it had denied ever seeing the skull, with or without a wig. It seemed obvious that someone had been playing a prank, but Jane wasn't sure how identifying the person behind the skull—given that he or she had been dead over a hundred years—would help discover who'd put it on the rack.

The sheriff, Sloan Trent, had wanted to send the skull off to the Smithsonian or the FBI lab, but the mayor had insisted it should stay in Lily until an identification had been made. So, Sloan had requested help from his old friend, Logan Raintree, head of Jane's Texas Krewe unit of the FBI teams of paranormal investigators known as the Krewe of Hunters. And that had led to Logan's asking Jane, whose specialty was forensic art, to come here. The medical examiner who'd seen the skull believed it was the skull of a woman and he had estimated that she'd been dead for a hundred to a hundred and fifty years.

"Come, Ms.—or, I guess it's Agent—Everett!" Henri said, pushing open the slatted doors and escorting her into the Gilded Lily. "Jennie! Come meet our forensic artist!"

Jane tried to take in the room while a slender woman wearing a flowered cotton dress came out from behind the long bar behind some tables to the left. The Gilded Lily, she quickly saw, was the real deal. She felt as if she'd stepped back in time. Of course, her first case with her Krewe—the second of three units—had been in her own hometown of San Antonio and had actually centered on an old saloon. But the Gilded Lily was a theater *and* a saloon or bar, and like nothing she'd ever seen before. The front tables were ready for poker players, with period furniture that was painstakingly rehabbed. To the right of the entry, an open pathway led to the theater. Rich red velvet drapes, separating the bar area from the stage and audience section, were drawn back with golden cords. The theater chairs weren't what she would've expected. The original owners had aimed for an East Coast ambience, so they, too, were covered in red velvet. The stage, beyond the audience chairs, was broad and deep, allowing for large casts and complicated sets. She saw what appeared to be a real stagecoach on stage right and, over on stage left, reaching from the apron back stage rear, were railroad tracks.

"Hello, welcome!"

The woman who'd been behind the bar came around to the entry, smiling as she greeted Jane. She thrust out her a hand and there was steel in her grip. "I'm Jennie Layton, stage mother."

"Stage *mother*?" Jane asked, smiling.

Jennie laughed. "Stage manager. But they call me stage mother—with affection, I hope. I take care of our actors…and just about everything else!" she said.

"Oh, come now! I do my share of the work," Henri protested.

Jennie smiled. "At night, we have three bartenders, four servers and a barback. And we have housekeepers who come in, too, but as far as fulltime employees go, well, it's Henri and me. And we're delighted you agreed to stay here."

"I thought the theater history might help you in identifying the woman," Henri said.

"Thank you. That makes sense. And it's beautiful and unique."

"Lily *is* unique! And the Gilded Lily is the jewel in her crown," Henri said proudly.

"Well, come on up. We have you in the Sage McCormick suite," Jennie told her, beaming.

The name was familiar to Jane from her reading. "Sage McCormick was an actress in the late 1800s, right?"

"All our rooms are now named for famous actors or actresses who came out West to play at the Gilded Lily,"

Henri said. "Sage, yes—she was one of the finest. She was in *Antigone* and *Macbeth* and starred in a few other plays out here. She was involved in a wonderful and lascivious scandal, too—absolutely a divine woman." He seemed delighted with the shocking behavior of the Gilded Lily's old star. "I'll get your bag."

"Oh, I'm fine," Jane said, but Henri had grabbed it already.

"Tut, tut," he said. "You may be a very capable agent, Ms. Everett, but here in Lily…agent is agent!"

"Well, thank you, then," Jane said.

Jennie showed the way up the curving staircase. The landing led to a balcony in a horseshoe shape. Jane looked down at the bar over a carved wooden railing, then followed Jennie to the room at the far end of the horseshoe. This room probably afforded the most privacy, as there was only one neighbor.

"The Sage McCormick suite," Jennie said, opening the door with a flourish.

It was a charming room. The bed was covered with a quilt—flowers on white—and the drapes were a filmy white with a crimson underlay.

"Those doors are for your outdoor balcony. It overlooks the side street but also gives you a view of the main street, although obstructed, I admit," Jennie said.

"And the dressing room through here…" Henri entered with her bag, throwing open a door at the rear of the spacious room. "It's still a dressing room, with a lovely new bath. Nothing was really undone. The first bathrooms were put in during the 1910s. We've just updated. And, you'll note, this one retains a dressing table and these old wooden armoires. Aren't they gorgeous?"

They were. The matching armoires were oak, with the symbols of comedy and tragedy carved on each side and on the doors. "They were a gift to Sage when she was here," Henri said reverently. "A patron of the arts was so delighted that he had these made for her!"

Jane peeked beyond. The bathroom was recently updated and had a tiled shower and whirlpool bath. The color scheme throughout was crimson and white with black edging.

"This is really lovely. Thank you," Jane said again.

"It's our best suite!" Henri gestured expansively around him.

"How come neither of you are in here?" Jane asked, smiling. "And what about your stars? I don't want to put anyone out."

"Oh," Jennie said. "Our 'stars' tend to be superstitious. They're in the other rooms on this level." With a quick grin she added, "And Henri and I are quite happy in our own rooms..."

Jane waited for her to say more.

Henri spoke instead. "Sage McCormick..." His voice trailed off. "Well, theater folk are a superstitious bunch. I mean, you know about her, don't you?"

"I know a little," Jane said. "She disappeared, didn't she?"

"From this room," Jennie explained. "There's all kinds of speculation. Some people believe she was a laudanum addict, and that she wandered off and met with a bad end at the hands of outlaws or Indians. Laudanum was used like candy back then. Lord knows how many people died from overusing it. Like today's over-the-counter pills. Too much and—"

"And some people believe she simply left Lily with her new love—supposedly she intended to elope—and changed her identity," Henri said impatiently. "Prior to that, she'd met and married a local man and they had a child together."

"Really? But she still kept her room at the Gilded Lily?" Jane asked.

"Of course. She was the *star.*" Henri spoke as if this was all that needed to be said.

"Anyway, the last time anyone reported seeing her was when she retired to this room after a performance," Henri went on.

"Her esteemed rendition of *Antigone!*" Jennie said. "What about the husband? Was he a suspect?" Jane asked.

"Her husband was downstairs in the bar, waiting for her. He was with a group of local ranchers and businessmen. One of her costars went up to get her, and Sage was gone. Just...gone. No one could find her, and she was never seen again," Jennie told her.

"Oh, dear! You're not superstitious, are you?" Henri asked. "I understood that you're a forensic artist but a law enforcement official, too."

Jane nodded. "I'll be fine here."

"Well, settle in, then. And, please, when you're ready, come on down. We'll be in the theater—I'll be giving notes on last night's performance. Join us whenever you're ready."

"I wouldn't want to interrupt a rehearsal."

"Oh, you won't be interrupting. The show is going well. We opened a few weeks ago, but I have to keep my actors off the streets, you know? You'll get to meet the cast, although the crew won't be there. This is for the performers. As Jennie mentioned, the cast lives at the Gilded Lily while performing, so you'll meet your neighbors."

"Thank you," Jane said, and glanced at her watch. "Sheriff Trent is supposed to be picking me up. I'll be down in a little while."

"Oh! And here's your key," Henri said, producing an old metal key. "The only people here are the cast and crew—"

"And bartenders and servers and a zillion other people who've come to see the show or have a drink," Jennie added drily. "Use your key."

"I will," Jane promised.

Henri and Jennie left the room. Jane closed the door behind them and stood still, gazing around. "Hello?" she said softly. "If you're here, I look forward to meeting you, Sage. What a beautiful name, by the way."

There was no response to her words. She shrugged, opened her bag and began to take out her clothing, going into the dressing room to hang her things in one of the armoires. She placed her makeup bag on the dressing table there, walked into the bathroom and washed her face. Back in the bedroom, she set up her laptop on the breakfast table near the balcony. Never sure if a place would have WiFi, she always brought her own connector.

Jane decided she needed to know more about Sage McCormick, and keyed in the name. She was astounded by the number of entries that appeared before her eyes. She went to one of the encyclopedia sites, assuming she'd find more truth than scandal there.

Jane read through the information: Sage had been born in New York City, and despite her society's scorn for actresses and her excellent family lineage, she'd always wanted to act. To that end, she'd left a magnificent mansion near Central Park to pursue the stage. She'd sold the place when she became the last surviving member of her family. Apparently aware that her choice of profession would brand her as wanton, she lived up to the image, marrying one of her costars and then divorcing him for the embrace of a stagehand. She flouted convention—but was known to be kind to everyone around her. She had been twenty-five when she'd come out to the Gilded Lily in 1870. By that point, she'd already appeared in numerous plays in New

York, Chicago and Boston. Critics and audiences alike had adored her. In Lily, she'd instantly fallen in love with local entrepreneur Alexander Cahill, married him almost immediately—and acted her way through the pregnancy that had resulted in the birth of her only child, Lily Cahill. On the night of May 1, 1872, after a performance of *Antigone*, Sage had gone to her room at the Gilded Lily Theater and disappeared from history. It was presumed that she'd left her husband and child to escape with a new lover, an outlaw known as Red Marston, as Red disappeared that same evening and was never seen in Lily again, nor did any reports of him ever appear elsewhere. Her contemporaries believed that the pair had fled to Mexico to begin their lives anew.

"Interesting," Jane murmured aloud. "So, Sage, did you run across the border and live happily ever after?"

She heard the old-fashioned clock on the dresser tick and nothing else. And she remembered that she'd promised to go downstairs. The sheriff was due to pick her up in thirty minutes, so if she was going to meet the cast, she needed to move.

Running into the dressing room, she ran her brush through her hair, then hurried out. As she opened the door to exit into the hall, she was startled to see a slim, older woman standing there with a tray in her hands. The tray held a small plug-in coffeepot, and little packs of coffee, tea, creamers and sugar.

"Hello!" the woman said. She looked at Jane as though terrified.

"Hi, I'm Jane Everett. Come on in, and thank you."

The woman swallowed. "I—I—I... Please don't make me go in that room!" she said.

Jane tried not to smile. "Let me take that, then. It's fine. You don't have to come in."

The woman pressed the tray into Jane's arms, looking vastly relieved. Jane brought it in and set it on the dresser. She'd find a plug in the morning.

When she turned around, the woman was still standing there. She wore a blue dress and apron and had to be one of the housekeepers.

"Thank you," Jane said again.

Suddenly, the woman stuck out her hand. "I'm Elsie Coburn. If you need anything, just ask me."

"Elsie, nice to meet you," Jane said, shaking her hand. She couldn't help asking, "How did this room get so clean?"

"Oh." Elsie blushed and glanced down. "I make the two girls clean this room. They do it together. They're okay as long as they don't work alone. Bess was in here one day and the door slammed on her and none of us could open it. Then it opened on its own, so...well, we don't have to clean it that often, you know? No one stays in this room. One of those ghost shows brought a cast and crew in here and the producer was going to stay in the room all night but he ran out.... People don't stay in that room. They just don't."

"Oh, well, I'm sorry that my coming here caused distress."

Elsie shook her head. "No, no, we're happy to have you. If you don't mind...please don't mention that you had to bring your own tray in."

"Of course not," Jane assured her. "Why did the producer of the ghost show run out in the middle of the night?"

"He said *she* was standing over his bed, that she touched him, that—"

"She? You mean Sage McCormick?" Elsie nodded.

"But what made him think she wanted to hurt him?"

"What?" Elsie was obviously mystified.

Jane smiled. "I thought ghost shows tried to prove that

places were haunted."

"This whole *town* is haunted. Bad things, really bad things, have happened over the years. The ghost-show people got all kinds of readings on their instruments. And the Old Jail next door! People leave there, too, even though they don't get their money back if they do. This place is…it's scary, Agent Everett. Very scary."

"But you live and work here," Jane said gently.

"I'm from here, and I don't tease the ghosts. I respect them. They're on Main Street, and they're all around. I keep my eyes glued to where I'm going, and that's it. I do my work and I go home, and if I hear a noise, I go the other way." She rubbed her hands on her apron. "Well, a pleasure to meet you. And we're glad you're here."

"Me, too. And don't worry about cleaning the room—no one has to clean it while I'm here. I'll just ask you to bring me fresh towels every couple of days. How's that?"

Elsie looked as if she might kiss her.

She nodded vigorously. "Thank you, miss. Thank you. I mean, thank you, Agent Everett."

"Jane is fine."

Flushing, Elsie said, "Jane." She turned and disappeared down the hall, heading for the stairs. Jane closed her door, locking it behind her as she'd been told to do.

On behalf of 1001 Dark Nights,
Liz Berry and M.J. Rose would like to thank ~

Doug Scofield

Steve Berry

Richard Blake

Dan Slater

Asha Hossain

Chris Graham

Kim Guidroz

BookTrib After Dark

Jillian Stein

and Simon Lipskar

45780219R00081

Made in the USA
Lexington, KY
09 October 2015